He looked like a guy who could break your heart just by smiling at you.

"Why are you going to Edinburgh?" she asked.

"I'm on holiday."

Everything she'd read about in mom's journal had painted Scotland as such an open and friendly place. Beautiful, rugged country; generous, warm people.

Her mother's people. She sighed.

Bobby Finn reached over and touched her knee. She glanced at his hand, so strong and firm.

The truth was, his touch grounded her a bit.

"You said you're with Scotland Yard—"

"Was. I've taken a leave to do some private work."

"What kind of private work?"

"I work for a team of private investigators, an international group that takes on unsolvable crimes. Quite fun, actually, when things work out."

"And when things don't work out?"

The intensity of his dark eyes touched her heart. She couldn't look away.

"When things don't work out, I get sent on holiday."

PAT WHITE

MISS FAIRMONT *and the* GENTLEMAN INVESTIGATOR

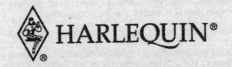

HARLEQUIN®

TORONTO • NEW YORK • LONDON
AMSTERDAM • PARIS • SYDNEY • HAMBURG
STOCKHOLM • ATHENS • TOKYO • MILAN • MADRID
PRAGUE • WARSAW • BUDAPEST • AUCKLAND

This book is dedicated to Heather Davis Koenig,
talented writer and good friend.

ISBN-13: 978-0-373-69247-7
ISBN-10:   0-373-69247-1

MISS FAIRMONT AND THE GENTLEMAN INVESTIGATOR

www.eHarlequin.com

Printed in U.S.A.

ABOUT THE AUTHOR

Growing up in the Midwest, Pat White has been spinning stories in her head ever since she was a little girl, stories filled with mystery, romance and adventure. Years later, while trying to solve the mysteries of raising a family in a house full of men, she started writing romantic fiction. After six Golden Heart nominations and a *Romantic Times BOOKreviews* award for Best Contemporary Romance (2004), her passion for storytelling and love of a good romance continues to find a voice in her tales of romantic suspense. Pat now lives in the Pacific Northwest, and she's still trying to solve the mysteries of living in a house full of men—with the added complication of two silly dogs and three spoiled cats. She loves to hear from readers, so please visit her at www.patwhitebooks.com.

Books by Pat White

HARLEQUIN INTRIGUE
944—SILENT MEMORIES
968—THE AMERICAN TEMP AND THE BRITISH INSPECTOR*
974—THE ENGLISH DETECTIVE AND THE ROOKIE AGENT*
980—MISS FAIRMONT AND THE GENTLEMAN INVESTIGATOR*

*The Blackwell Group

CAST OF CHARACTERS

Bobby Finn—Investigator for the Blackwell Group, Bobby resents his assignment playing babysitter to a spoiled American girl in the UK, especially when she denies she's in danger.

Grace Fairmont—Her mother died when she was a baby, and Grace is on a soul-searching mission to find herself by touring Mom's homeland of Scotland. She never expects to encounter danger on her trip.

Max Templeton—Director of the Blackwell Group—a private investigative team hired to protect Grace Fairmont while she tours the UK.

Harry Franklin—Seems like a gentleman when he helps Grace after she's knocked down at King's Cross railway station. Yet appearances can be deceiving.

Uncle Gerry, Aunt Rose, Cousin Anne and Cousin Jimmy—The family Grace aches to meet. She hopes they will give her answers about her mother's mysterious life in Scotland.

Chapter One

"So, who is she?" Art McDonald said. "A murder suspect? Thief, what?"

Bobby Finn glanced at his former Scotland Yard partner then to his assignment: American Grace Fairmont, helpless rich girl whose father didn't want her traveling the U.K. alone.

She sat across the pub from Bobby and Art, leafing through travel brochures and analyzing maps. This was a fancy holiday for her, a diversion from her dull life.

For Bobby, this was a jail sentence. He'd jeopardized the Blackwell Group's last case, and he'd been sent back to London as punishment. A private dick working as a babysitter.

"She's a bloody schoolteacher," Bobby explained. "And a thorn in my side."

"A school teacher?" Art said. "What's she done?"

"Besides bore me to tears?" Bobby swallowed

back his ale. "She's nothing, Art. She's not a suspect or an informant."

"I think you're overreacting, mate."

"I should be back in the States, working on a murder case for Blackwell. Instead, I'm stuck following that female around for two weeks."

Miss Grace Fairmont had been sitting at a table in the corner for nearly an hour. Her shoulder-length blond hair floated about round cheeks that made her look more like a teenager than a twenty-six-year-old woman. She wore a denim jacket, a purple scarf and soft pink lipstick, accentuating full lips, lips that looked too sexy to be on such a youthful face. A shopping bag sat by her side carrying her spoils from a prestigious lingerie shop.

Bobby had spent the day following a woman on her shopping spree. Could there be a harsher sentence?

"It's great to see you," Art said, leaning across the table. "Tell me about Blackwell, give me all the details."

Details of a missing boy, almost lost forever thanks to Bobby?

"I cocked-up, mate. That's why they sent me back."

"You know Max wouldn't punish you for being human. We all make mistakes, Bobby."

Yeah, but Bobby more than most, right? What made him think he could shake his past? Bobby was a failure at protection. Why had Max picked him for this assignment?

"Bobby?"

He glanced at Art, his mate from the Special Crimes Initiative at Scotland Yard. Art was a good friend, a mentor, and Bobby had missed him. He wished Art had stayed with the private investigative team back in the States, but the man had a wife and kids. He had a life.

Bobby envied him.

"What happened?" Art pushed.

"We were investigating a case of a missing boy." Bobby leaned forward in the booth. "I looked right into the bastard's eyes, Paul Reynolds was his name, and I didn't realize he was the man who was demanding the ransom." He hesitated and shook his head. "What the hell's the matter with me?"

"Nothing, it happens to all of us. We misjudge people."

"Not Max, he doesn't make mistakes."

"He's human, Bobby, just like the rest of us. And consider what he had to struggle with to get back on his feet. I can see why you admire him, but don't put him on a pedestal. He wouldn't like it."

He couldn't help it. Max was the man who'd challenged Bobby out of a life of crime and pushed him into a career in law enforcement. Max was Bobby's only father figure, although only ten years his senior. Max had encouraged Bobby, given him a chance.

And Bobby had let him down.

"I was doing it by the book, asking the right questions, digging for secrets. I've watched Barnes. He's so analytical and I thought I could learn from him. It all fell into place when Reynolds helped me draw my conclusions."

Bobby had been trusting and gullible. Just like when he'd trusted his mum to come back for him. Bobby should have known she couldn't stand the sight of him, not after what he'd done.

"The man had no criminal background?" Art asked.

"None. He was an upstanding citizen."

"Then you had no reason to suspect him. People lie, Bobby. You can't control that."

"But I don't have to believe them."

Art took a sip of ale.

"The odd thing was," Bobby continued, "even as I drove off with the information Reynolds gave me, feeling all proud of myself..." Bobby hesitated.

"Even as you drove off, what?"

Bobby looked into Art's gray-blue eyes. "I got this feeling, like something wasn't right, like there was something off about Reynolds."

"But you didn't act on that feeling?"

"It's a feeling, mate. Not proof of anything. Barnes always says—"

"Screw Barnes."

"I'd rather not, thanks."

Art smiled. "Barnes has his way of working cases

and you have yours. Max always thought you'd make an excellent investigator because you were able to get into the devilish mind of a criminal."

Sure he could. It was his mind, as well.

"Stop thinking so much and follow your gut," Art said.

The waitress served their fish and chips.

"Ah, my gut's been missing this," Bobby joked. He forked a piece of fish and took a bite. Closing his eyes, he moaned with appreciation. There were some things about London he missed desperately.

And others he was glad to leave behind, like the shame of his past.

"Uh, Bobby?" Art said.

Bobby opened his eyes as he savored the taste.

"You'd better eat fast. It looks like your girl is leaving."

Bobby glanced at Grace Fairmont's table. Blast, she was handing her waitress her credit card.

"Bloody hell," he muttered, glancing at his full plate of food.

"We'll get the waitress to box it," Art offered.

Bobby pulled out his wallet.

"Don't even try it," Art said, not looking at him.

Art hailed a waitress and asked for a box. Bobby kept his eyes trained on Grace Fairmont. This was going to be torture, for sure, more waiting while she shopped for sexy nightgowns and bras.

Unbeknownst to Miss Fairmont, her father had

hired Blackwell to protect her while on her trip. She was a schoolteacher with a steady boyfriend; she lived an unremarkable life in a suburb of Chicago.

Still, Max had given Bobby the directive: *Follow her. Protect her.*

From what? Abusing her bloody credit cards?

She signed her receipt and grabbed her things: a small red suitcase, light-gray backpack and shopping bag. She headed for the door.

"It was great catching up." Bobby shook Art's hand. He watched Grace leave the pub and head west in the direction of more shopping.

Art smiled. "Remember what I said."

"Yeah, I'll be sure to tell Barnes you think we're made for each other," Bobby joked, heading for the door. The waitress handed him his box of fish and chips.

"Behave," Art called after him.

"What, are you kidding?"

GRACE FAIRMONT waited at King's Cross Station for the 6:00 p.m. train to Edinburgh.

This was it.

The beginning of her journey to find answers.

She leaned against a wall to do some people-watching. Everyone looked so absorbed in their worlds. A mother knelt down and pointed to the schedule board. Her daughter, maybe six, looked up, eyes wide, so trusting and innocent.

Grace snapped her gaze from the mother and child and caught sight of a man, racing across the station, looking for someone. Maybe his lover?

She thought about Steven back in Chicago, about what he'd be like as a husband and a father—wonderful, attentive, loyal. For some reason, that gave her little peace.

What on earth was the matter with her? Steven was a great guy, a little over-protective, like Dad, but he meant well.

Yet Grace could not give herself completely until she understood herself better; understood herself by walking in her mother's footsteps.

Her mother, whom she'd never known.

Grace Fairmont needed to exorcise her ghosts and heal that empty spot in her heart. She needed answers and was convinced this trip to the United Kingdom would bring her closure somehow.

Dad had argued with her, told Grace it was a waste of time, that she was only torturing herself. But once he knew she was determined to do her soul-searching, he relented and gave her a treasured gift: a journal her mom had left behind.

Grace had wondered why Dad had never shared it with her all these years. When she asked him, he said he was trying to protect her, once again, from hurt and pain. That seemed to be his primary focus in life: to protect his little girl.

But Grace wasn't little anymore, and she ached to stand on her own.

Grace had coveted Mom's journal, filled with private thoughts about her life and her family.

About her baby girl.

She wrote with such love on those pages. Yet she'd only known Grace for a year before being killed by a drunk driver.

Grace shook off the melancholy and headed for the train, anxious to get away and clear her head. If nothing else, this could be a good diversion from her routine life.

She'd always been routine, accountable, the perfect daughter, probably because she didn't want to risk losing the love of her only parent. Then, after Dad had married Andrea, she'd worked hard to please her stepmother, as well.

But inside something had always felt off, crooked.

Which is what started this self-identity quest.

Passengers began to board the train for Edinburgh. She lined up, feeling a little claustrophobic. At only five foot three inches, she tended to feel that way when surrounded by a large group of people. It was even more hilarious when her eighth-grade science students towered over her.

She let her gaze wander to the passengers boarding the next car: couples holding hands and families beginning a holiday in Scotland.

Some day, she thought. Some day she'd have a family and take trips with her children. Grace would always be there for her—

SMACK!

Something slammed into her, knocking her off balance. She braced her fall with her hand and pain shot up her arm. Adrenaline rushed to her head as she struggled to catch her breath. She looked up to see three teenage boys whizzing away on skateboards, security officers chasing after them.

Someone touched her shoulder.

"You okay, miss?"

She glanced up at a businessman in a gray suit with an angular face and blue eyes.

"Fine, I think," she said.

He pulled her to her feet, his hand pinching her arm. He was trying to be helpful and didn't realize the grip he had on her.

"Thanks," she said.

"Those boys should be strung up for knocking you down."

"They're kids," she excused, knowing how energetic teenagers were.

"Yes, well, they should have better sense."

Now he sounded like her father.

"Please." He motioned for her to board ahead of him.

She climbed onto the train, shooting him one last smile of thanks, and made for the first-class section.

She wanted to be pampered, to have someone take care of *her* for a change.

It had been so long since she'd put herself first. She'd spent her life worrying about Dad, her step-mom, her half sisters, Annie and Claire, and even her students at Inglewood Junior High.

Grace found a seat and settled by the window so she could get a view of the ocean as they got closer to Newcastle.

The helpful businessman took a seat across from her.

"Are you on holiday, then?" he asked.

So much for peace and quiet.

WHAT'S THIS? The boring American girl had already snagged a new boyfriend?

Bobby had chosen a seat a few rows down, watching the bloke in the suit make conversation with Grace.

Bobby sensed it was an effort for her to respond. Why? Was she the unsociable type? Or did she sense something creepy about the man? Bobby had. Nonsense, she wouldn't have given him so much of her time if that were the case. They'd chatted on and off for nearly half the trip to Edinburgh.

Bugger, they were headed to Scotland and Bobby hadn't had time to grab his things from the hotel. He'd have to buy some new clothes, courtesy of Blackwell.

Bobby eyed Miss Fairmont's train companion. The man wore an expensive suit and a gold earring, but worn, cheap trainers. There was something off about him. The bloke was working too hard to charm Miss Fairmont.

Why? Sure, she was mildly attractive, but not a model type who would draw the attention of a hoity-toity like suit man over there.

It made him ill to watch the businessman lean toward her, whisper a joke and laugh at it himself. She shot him a strained smile and pressed her forehead to the window. She looked as if she wanted to jump to get away from him.

How could he be so blind?

A few minutes passed. The suit glanced at Bobby, who refocused on newspaper headlines: the Prime Minister had struck a deal with the French regarding nuclear power; G8 aid pledges were not meeting expectations; a new program was in the works to improve students' handwriting.

When Bobby glanced up, Grace was heading into the next car. What's this? Was she finally getting away from the wanker, or just making a trip to the toilet?

Five minutes passed. Ten. The suit checked his watch, looked impatient. It was almost as if he was afraid she'd left for good. The bloke stood and went into the next train car.

Bobby folded his newspaper. Suit man's interest in Grace was beyond obsessive.

Follow her. Protect her.

Bobby went into the next train car in search of Grace and her suitor. It was half-full, but there was no sign of the girl or the businessman.

What could this be about? A random stalker? More like a prick who couldn't take no for an answer.

Bobby pushed through to the next car. The conductor announced they were approaching Newcastle. The train slowed and Bobby held on to the back of a seat as his weight shifted with the motion of the brake.

A few passengers stood and gathered their things, blocking his view of the next car.

The train stopped, passengers got off and the doors closed. Bobby glanced out the window and spotted the businessman racing across the platform. Had Grace gotten off the train and he was following her?

Bloody hell.

The train pulled away and Bobby raced through the car peering through windows, trying to catch sight of her. This was all wrong. Her father had said she planned a trip to Edinburgh, where she'd start her tour of Scotland.

This was supposed to be an easy assignment: follow and protect a girl. How hard could that be?

For you, bloody impossible.

He pushed through another car, peered out the

window and spotted the businessman march down the steps, out of sight.

Bobby pounded his fist against the back of a seat. He'd cocked-up in less than twenty-four hours. Max wouldn't be able to ignore this one.

And Bobby couldn't ignore the voices in his head: *How could you let this happen? Of course your mother didn't want you.*

The sound of muffled tapping drew his attention to the back of the car. It was coming from the toilet.

He went to the door and knocked. "Anyone in there?"

A woman's whimpers echoed through the door.

Blast. The door couldn't be locked unless she'd locked it. And if that were the case, why hadn't she let herself out of there. Was she bound or worse?

"Miss? I'm going to push open the door," he said.

He cracked open the door and she blinked back at him through teary eyes, a white handkerchief stuck in her mouth, her wrists bound with flex cuffs.

"Good God," he hushed. "Here." He helped her to a seat. She shook with fear.

"Let's get this off you." He pulled the gag from her mouth, guilt ripping him up inside.

He let this happen. Wasn't there to protect her. Again.

"He t-t-took." She could barely speak without stuttering.

"Shh. Have a rest."

"He took…my mom," she said.

"It's okay, you're okay now."

He pulled out his pocketknife to cut her bindings.

"Hold it right there," a male voice said behind him.

Chapter Two

Bobby's hands went up and he glanced over his shoulder. A bloke holding Met Police identification in one hand and a gun in the other towered over him. Relief that it wasn't the businessman was quickly replaced by shame. Old, bitter memories tore at his chest.

You're a bad seed, a delinquent who will spend his life in prison.

No, things were different now; Bobby was one of the good guys.

"I'm trying to help," Bobby said.

The officer glanced at Bobby's hand. "By threatening her with a knife?"

"I was going to cut her loose."

He held the man's gaze, struggling to keep the guilt from his eyes. Guilt for the many sins he had yet to be absolved of; guilt for letting the stranger hurt the American Grace.

"Hand over the knife."

Bobby did as ordered, very slowly. "I'm a former inspector with Scotland Yard."

"And I'm Prince William." The cop pocketed the knife. "Stand up, arms behind your head."

"No," Grace said.

Bobby studied her as she addressed the officer.

"He helped me," she said. "He's not the bad guy."

The officer eyed Bobby, who fought off buried shame and held his gaze.

"How about some identification?" the officer asked.

"Cut her free first."

The policeman holstered his gun and pulled out his own pocketknife. Grace raised her bound wrists and he cut them loose. She rubbed the skin, raw from the unforgiving plastic.

"ID," Bobby said, handing him his driver's license and Blackwell business card.

"Robert Finn."

"Bobby," he corrected.

The detective eyed it and nodded. "You used to be with Scotland Yard? Doing what?"

"I was an inspector with the Special Crimes Initiative."

"And you left because?"

"Shouldn't you be more worried about this woman than my employment history?"

Bobby didn't want him wasting time trying to analyze his motives; he was furious about the girl's attack and he wanted answers.

Considering her teary eyes and trembling fingers, he wasn't sure if *she* had any.

"Miss?" the detective said.

"Grace, Grace Fairmont."

"Miss Fairmont, I'm Detective Adam Parker with the Metro Police. Can you tell me what happened?"

"A man," she started, then paused. "He was sitting by me, making conversation. A stranger…" Her voice trailed off.

"I saw him get off the train at Newcastle," Bobby offered.

The detective narrowed his eyes at him.

"I noticed how he pushed himself on the girl. Something about the bloke didn't sit right."

The detective redirected his attention to Grace. "What did you talk about?"

"The weather, London, my trip. He said his name was Harry Franklin, Esquire."

She glanced at her fingers, fiddling with a ring she wore on her right hand. She was keeping something private, to herself. Bobby could sense it.

"He asked me a lot of questions," she continued. "I tried pretending to be asleep, but he didn't get the message. I…I excused myself and went to another car, hoping he'd leave me alone."

She coughed and Bobby wanted to reach out and comfort her. But he, too, was a stranger and after what had just happened he knew she'd most likely recoil from the gesture.

."He followed me," she said. "And I got this feeling." She looked up at the detective. "Like he was going to hurt me. So I went into the bathroom, but he shoved the door open and pressed himself up against me and…" She waved her hand, then placed her fingers to her mouth, as if to fight off sobs.

Bobby fisted his right hand, wanting to find the bastard and break his nose. If he had touched her inappropriately— "What did he do to you?" Bobby said. He couldn't stop himself.

"No," she said. "Nothing like that."

She held his gaze, her clear blue eyes penetrating and intense as if she could see into his soul. Bobby snapped his attention to the detective.

"It's okay, now, miss," Detective Parker consoled. "He's gone, he's off the train according to Mr. Finn." The detective knelt beside her. "Your attacker can't hurt you anymore. But I'd like to call in a description to the Transport Police."

She nodded and cleared her throat. "He was tall—"

"About six two," Bobby offered.

"Short, trim hair, blue eyes, this one," she pointed to her right eye, "had a brown spot by the pupil. He had an accent, but it wasn't like yours, Detective." She glanced at Bobby. "It was more like yours."

He'd called Dublin his home until his mother had sent him to live with Uncle Thomas in London. Had she recognized an Irish accent?

"What else?" Detective Parker prompted.

"He had a gold earring in his left ear," Bobby said. "And he wore an expensive suit, maybe Armani, but not his shoes," Bobby said, puzzling for a second. "The bloke wore trainers, beat-up trainers."

"Did he say anything to you when he assaulted you in the bathroom?" Parker asked her.

"He said 'You can't run like your mother.'" She glanced up at the detective. "But I never even knew my mother. She died when I was a year old."

"Mistaken identity?" Bobby said to the detective.

"Sounds like. How about your luggage?"

"He took my backpack."

"But he wasn't carrying it when I saw him on the platform," Bobby added.

"It might still be on the train," Parker said. "I'll start a search after I radio in."

"I didn't know they put Metro detectives on the rail system," Bobby said.

"They don't. Lucky for you I'm on my way to meet family in Edinburgh."

"Very lucky," Bobby added, nodding at Grace.

"I'm going to call it in, then search for your pack." He glanced at Bobby. "Could use a hand if you're interested."

"No," she said again, reaching out to Bobby.

Her hand landed on the sleeve of his leather jacket. "I'd rather he stay here, with me."

She looked at him with such trust, such gratitude…and for a second, he welcomed her confidence. Then he remembered why he was here: as an employee, hired by her father.

Mr. Fairmont had specifically said he didn't want his daughter finding out he'd hired Blackwell. He feared she'd be furious and would try to shake off the secret bodyguard.

"It's okay," she said to Bobby after watching him for a moment. "You don't have to stay with me."

She must have read the internal struggle in his eyes.

Bugger, he'd always been so good at hiding his demons behind a layer of smiles and charm.

"I'll sit with you." He smiled.

Relief eased the tension lines on her face.

"I'll check back." The detective left.

"Your cheek is red," Bobby said. "Let me get you some ice."

He started to get up but she grabbed his jacket sleeve. "No, please, would you mind staying here and talking to me?"

"Of course."

She glanced out the window, hugging her midsection.

"Are you chilled?" he said.

She shook her head that she wasn't. She looked absorbed in the landscape, yet there was nothing to see outside but the black horizon of the North Sea.

He studied her young features: round cheeks and freckles dotting her slightly upturned nose. She wore little makeup to speak of, but her cheeks were a natural rose color, so she really didn't need it. She'd look fourteen if it weren't for something wary in her eyes and a full lower lip that gave her a natural pout.

She had plenty to pout about. She'd been accosted on a train in a strange country. How could she let the bastard get the advantage? Didn't the girl have any protective instincts?

"What did you mean, he took your mum?" Bobby asked.

She sighed and seemed to melt into the seat.

"He ripped my locket off my neck. It had a picture of my mom and my dad."

It was the only photograph she had of her, Grace realized. She closed her eyes and fought back more tears. No, she wasn't a fragile girl who'd fall apart because she'd been mugged. People were mugged all the time. They survived. She would.

But it wasn't the mugging that tore at her heart. That photograph of her mother had been Grace's only link to her, her only connection.

"Aw, come on, love, it's not that bad. I'm sure your father can find you another."

The man in the black leather jacket had such a calming nature. She couldn't help but be drawn to him.

To think when she'd noticed him earlier on the

train, she'd thought him rough and dangerous. It was the intensity of his dark eyes whenever he glanced her way that made her nervous. That and his two days' growth of beard.

He looked like a tough guy, a guy who could break your heart by smiling at you.

How could she have known that Bobby Finn was the kind man, and Harry was the danger?

"He seemed nice," she blurted out.

"Who, the hoity-toity bloke sitting next to you?"

"Yeah."

And he did. He'd helped her up after she'd been knocked down by the teenagers and he'd sat by her on the train as if protecting her.

Could she have worse instincts?

"Gawd, I'm so stupid," she muttered.

"Don't go beating yourself up, miss. When someone's nice to you there's no reason to think he's going to hurt you. Still…" He hesitated and rubbed at his beard. "He *was* prepared, wasn't he? He carried ties and a gag on him like women carry handbags?"

"He's a lawyer." She wasn't sure what that had to do with anything.

"Well, that explains it then." He smiled, his cheek dimpling.

She almost felt herself smile.

"You sure you didn't know him?" he asked.

"No, I've never seen him before today."

"And he didn't say anything besides the comment about your mum?"

"No." Her gaze drifted to the center aisle of the train.

She wasn't sure why she lied, other than she didn't want to impose on this man's kindness. What purpose would it serve to tell him about the other comment, the one about the dangers of a single girl traveling north of Edinburgh?

That threat was meant for someone else. He'd obviously mistaken her for another woman traveling alone to Scotland. It had to be. Grace didn't have enemies, no one who'd threaten her life.

Everything she'd read in Mom's journal had painted Scotland as such an open and friendly place. Beautiful, rugged country; generous, warm people.

Her mother's people. She sighed.

"Whoa there, love." Bobby Finn reached over and touched her knee.

She glanced at his hand, so strong and firm.

He snapped it back. "Sorry. You looked so sad like you'd lost your dog or something."

Or something.

"It's okay," she whispered. "I'm really tired, I guess."

The truth was, his touch grounded her a bit. She should be ashamed of herself for so willingly accepting comfort from yet another stranger.

A stranger she knew nothing about.

"Why are you going to Edinburgh?" she asked.

"I'm on holiday."

"You said you're with Scotland Yard—"

"Was. I've taken a leave to do some private work."

"What kind of private work?"

"Twenty questions, is it?" he said with a smile.

She shook her head. "I'm sorry."

"Don't be. You're wary, you should be. Okay then, I work for a team of private investigators, an international group that takes on unsolvable crimes. Quite fun, actually, when things work out." He glanced at his fingers, loosely interlaced in his lap.

"And when things don't work out?"

He looked her straight in the eye. The intensity of those dark eyes touched her heart. She couldn't look away.

"When things don't work out, I get sent on holiday." He smiled, but it looked forced, as if there was great pain behind his words.

"I'm sorry," she said.

"Don't be. I haven't taken a break in over ten years. I could use a little sightseeing, tour the castles and walk the battlegrounds."

"Culloden?"

"That tops the list."

She nodded. A few minutes passed.

"What else are you going to do?" she said, to distract herself. She'd been attacked, in a strange country, in a public place. She'd suddenly wondered if Dad was right to be so protective, right when he'd said she was incapable of taking care of herself.

No, she'd lived with his overprotectiveness for years, and she finally needed to get away on her own, find some answers about her mother.

"I'll probably head up to Inverness," Bobby Finn said. "Make some stops in between, play golf. Haven't finalized everything."

"What's Edinburgh like?"

"What, you've never been?"

"No."

"Make sure you tour Edinburgh Castle and Holyrood."

"I'm only going to be there a day. I'm not much for big cities."

"You might be able to do both in a day." His enthusiastic smile faded. "Hold on, I'm such a bloody sod. That bastard lawyer got your money and your credit cards, didn't he?"

"Yeah, but at least he didn't get my suitcase. I checked it with the guard's van before getting on board." She sighed with relief. He hadn't taken her prized possession: Mom's journal, the roadmap Grace would use to make this journey.

Bobby Finn leaned forward in his seat and pulled out his wallet. "Do you need money? I think I've got a few hundred pounds in here."

"No, don't." She placed her hand to his. The intimate connection warmed her fingertips. "I'll be

fine. I'll wire my…" Who? If she wired Dad she'd
have to tell him the whole story. He'd demand Grace
come home, they'd get in another big fight. And
Steven? He'd practically followed her onto the plane
he wanted to come with her so badly.

This was something she needed to do alone.

"I'll be fine," she said. She realized her fingers
still touched the back of his hand. He slipped his
hand from hers and shoved his wallet back into his
pocket. She studied this tough-looking man whose
eyes warmed with tenderness.

"I'm hot-blooded," he said.

"Excuse me?"

"When you touched me you noticed how hot my
skin was?"

Actually, she thought it was a combination of
coming off an adrenaline rush and needing a friendly
connection.

"My temperature runs about two degrees above
normal. You know, hot-blooded, hot-headed. At least
that was the excuse they came up with in school."

Chatting with him was a nice diversion. It distracted Grace from the violent flashes of being assaulted. She could pretend to be normal again and
deny feeling victimized.

"Did you get in trouble a lot?" she said.

"Every bloody day. I was ba-a-ad."

"I doubt that."

His gaze snapped up to meet hers. He looked

frightened for a second. Then his lips curved into a mischievous grin.

"I was so bad I was expelled from three primary schools," he said.

"And yet you became a policeman."

His smile faded. He looked almost embarrassed.

The door opened and Detective Parker stepped up to her. "No sign of your backpack, yet, miss."

"Thanks. At least I've got my cell phone. Kept it in my jacket."

"Is there someone you can phone when you get to Edinburgh?"

No way around it. She'd have to call Steven to wire her money. She'd make him promise not to tell Dad what had happened. "I have a friend I can call."

"You're sure? Because I could always front you a few pounds."

"I already tried that," Bobby said. "She won't take money from strangers." He winked.

"Hey, taking help from a stranger got me into this mess in the first place," she said.

"How's that, miss?" Detective Parker asked.

"That man, Harry, helped me after I was knocked down by teenagers at the train station."

"This feels like a set-up," the detective said. "He probably paid those boys to knock you over so he could get into your good graces and stay close to you."

"Why?" Her voice squeaked a pitch higher than usual. "What have I done to deserve this?"

"Nothing, you've done nothing wrong," Bobby said. "It's not your fault. They'll get the bastard."

"Transport Police will do their best," Parker offered. "They've notified Newcastle Police to be on the lookout. In the meantime, we don't have to worry about a repeat attack. He's miles away from Edinburgh. You're safe now."

Her attacker's warning echoed in her mind: *Traveling north of Edinburgh can be dangerous for a single girl.*

It was a hollow threat from a bully who picked on naive tourists. She'd be strong, gather her courage and finish what she came to do.

SHE LOOKED adorable when she slept, Bobby thought, studying Grace Fairmont's young features. She'd fallen asleep after an hour's worth of conversation with Bobby and Detective Parker, but most of it had been with Bobby. With every passing minute he sensed she grew more comfortable with him, more relaxed.

There was something open about her, yet fragile. A part of him wanted to shout in her face: *Don't trust me, I'm no good. I'm pretending to be something I'm not.*

And I obviously can't protect you.

But he couldn't for so many reasons, his position with Blackwell topping the list.

He'd been hired to do this simple job. If he wanted to make his way back to the Blackwell team in the

States, he needed to follow orders and make sure she got safely home from her holiday.

If he succeeded he could earn a bonus or maybe a higher spot on the team. There was a rumor that the Patron was going to start a second team and maybe Bobby could get in line for that promotion.

He glanced at the sweet-faced Miss Fairmont. Her safety was worth nothing but a promotion to him.

You really are a bastard, Finn.

Detective Parker returned from making a call. "Someone spotted the man she described leaving the train station. Transport Police did a background on Harry Franklin, but nothing turned up on their wanted lists."

"It's probably an alias," Bobby said, watching Grace sleep. Fitfully, of course. He guessed she was both exhausted by her experience and terrified, as well.

"What do you make of it?" Parker said, eyeing Bobby. "Simple mugging or something more?"

"Sounds like a case of mistaken identity, but feels like more, doesn't it?"

Parker nodded. "What do you know about her?"

"As much as you do," he lied. He didn't want to reveal his true assignment and complicate matters further. "She's a fragile one."

And a bit secretive. Bobby sensed the American wasn't being completely truthful about the attack. Why? What was she hiding?

He'd read her file and had become familiar with the life of Grace Fairmont. An only child, her father raised her by himself until she turned eight, when he married. Grace was a straight-A student, a high achiever, yet instead of pursuing business she opted to teach science to teenagers.

Bobby couldn't understand it. He remembered what teenagers were like: emotionally fractured, insecure and angry. Why would anyone choose to be around that day in and day out?

He didn't understand her choice of careers any more than he understood today's attack. There was definitely more to it than a random mugging. After all, the bloke had used flex cuffs and knew exactly how to subdue her without drawing unwanted attention. He'd timed it perfectly.

Bobby's ground his teeth at the thought of Grace being seriously injured while under his watchful eye.

He wouldn't let that happen.

Yet he couldn't protect her if he didn't have her whole story. He stood and pulled out his mobile.

"I'll be right back," he said to Parker.

He went in between cars and called Eddie, Blackwell's computer expert.

"Eddie Malone."

"Hey, mate, it's Bobby."

"Bobby! Hey, it's Bobby from London," he called out to the rest of the team. "What's up, man?"

"I need background. Grace Fairmont."

"Our client's daughter? The one you're playing bodyguard for?"

At least he didn't call Bobby a babysitter.

"That's the one," Bobby said. "I want what the father might be keeping from us. Dig into the family's background, her job contacts, mates from college, that sort of thing."

"So, let me get this straight: you want me to investigate our client?"

"There's been a development and I need to know intimate details about Grace and the Fairmont family."

"Okee-dokee."

"Also, do a search for Harry Franklin, Esquire. It's probably an alias, but see what you can find. And…" He hesitated, not sure what compelled him to make the next request. "Get me everything you can on the girl's boyfriend, the name's in the file."

"This doesn't sound like a simple bodyguard job."

"Just trying to get the key players straight in my head, mate. Nothing covert."

"Wait, Max wants to talk to you."

Great. Max would hear the tension in Bobby's voice and inquire about his day.

"Bobby? How's the weather in London?"

"Actually, guv, I'm in Scotland. Taking the rail up to Edinburgh."

"Everything okay?"

Blast, did Max have such little faith in Bobby?

"Fine, guv, why?"

"I know this wasn't the assignment you'd hoped for. But I gave it to you because I trust you, Bobby. I know you'll take care of the girl."

"Well, actually, it got off to a rocky start. She was assaulted on the train."

"What? A random attack?"

"Looks that way." Bobby paused. "But it doesn't feel that way."

"Follow your instincts, Bobby. Trust them."

"Like I did with Paul Reynolds?"

"Let go of it, mate. He had everyone fooled, even his best friends. You said you thought he was too charming, too happy with the world. You knew something was wrong. You didn't trust yourself. Sometimes you have to look beyond the facts."

Like into Grace Fairmont's unsettled eyes?

"I'll press the father for more personal information," Max said. "Maybe he's keeping something from us."

"Thanks, guv." Bobby heard the door slide open behind him. He turned and spotted Grace holding her mobile in her hand.

"It's a good thing she's got you as her shadow, isn't it?" Max said.

"Sure. I've got to run."

"It's two weeks, Bobby. Then you'll be back with the team."

"Yes, sir." He ended the call and smiled at Grace. "Everything okay?"

"Yeah, Detective Parker said the reception's better out here." She motioned to her phone.

"I'll give you privacy, then." He brushed past her, and she touched his jacket sleeve.

"Thanks, again."

Glancing down into those green eyes of hers, Bobby read vulnerability, yet determination. But determination for what?

Bobby Finn went into the passenger car and sat down across from the policeman. Grace sighed. She'd been so lucky that both of them were on her train. They were the strength she needed to ground herself after the attack.

She gripped the metal pole as the memories flashed to the surface. She'd thought Harry a nice, albeit pushy, guy who needed attention. There was no indication that he was dangerous.

What did you expect, girl? It's not like you've got street smarts, what with your father hovering over you most of your life, protecting you, sheltering you.

If only Mom had been alive to balance things out, Dad wouldn't have been so smothering. Yet he was trying to make up for that empty spot in Grace's life where there should have been another parent.

A loving, nurturing mother.

"Enough," she said, trying to shove back her frustration. That's what this trip was about: Grace's personal elixir, a way to finally let go of the questions and confusion, a way to look ahead instead of dwelling in the past, dwelling in the sadness of not knowing her mom.

After she visited her mother's hometown, and toured some of the spots written about in her journal, Grace would start a new, fresh life.

At some point you have to let go.

Grace called Steven. She'd calmly tell him what happened and ask him to wire her a few hundred pounds until she could replace her credit cards. She had to do it in such a way that he wouldn't worry, or board the next British Airways flight to London.

Sometimes, between her father and Steven, she felt as though she was being suffocated.

Her call went into voice mail.

"Hey, Steven, it's Grace. I lost my wallet on the train to Scotland, can you believe it? Anyway, I was wondering if you could wire me some cash until I can get access to my bank account, just enough for a day or two. Sorry I have to ask. And don't worry about me. There's a former Scotland Yard inspector and Metro policeman on the train. They're taking care of me. Anyway, we'll be pulling into the station in a few minutes. You can reach me on my cell. Thanks."

She pressed End. Something at the bottom of the steps reflected back at her.

Her breath caught in her throat. Her locket. She

picked it up and rubbed the worn gold, its shine faded with age.

She opened it.

The picture of her mother was missing.

Chapter Three

Mom's photograph. Gone.

This trip was off to a horrible start for sure. First the mugging, now the missing picture. She wanted to call Dad and ask if he could send another, but then she'd have to tell him the whole ugly story. She wasn't in the mood for lectures.

She wanted a nice, quiet room where she could unwind, have a hot cup of tea and read through Mom's journal. Again.

At least she still had that. Thank God she'd packed it in her suitcase.

She slipped the phone into her pocket and went back to her seat.

"Everything okay?" Bobby asked.

Bobby, the private detective on holiday. She could use his help right about now.

No, she had to do this on her own, couldn't trust anyone, especially not a stranger.

"Good news, actually." She held out the locket. "Found my locket."

"Brilliant," Bobby said.

"Mom's picture is missing, though."

"Probably fell out when he dropped it," Detective Parker offered.

She squeezed it in her hand, the warmth of the metal easing the chill around her heart.

A heart that had never felt completely whole as a child without a mother.

She glanced at Bobby Finn whose eyes were intent on her. She was sure he could read her thoughts. Her gaze drifted out the window. She was anxious to reach the small town of Pitlochry where her mother had grown up.

But now it would take her a few days to get there. She had to cancel her credit cards and wait for their replacements so she could continue her trip.

She should call Dad, especially now that Steven knew something was up. Dad would probably lecture her about always keeping a stash of traveler's checks handy. But she'd been rushed at work, organizing material for her substitute. She'd barely made it to the airport on time. It was only thanks to practical Steven that she'd made her flight.

Steven, a nice, practical man, like her father. Not wild, passionate or unpredictable.

Steven was exactly the type of man she knew she'd marry.

Then why are you here, girl? Why didn't you stay home and marry the guy?

Good question. And one of many.

They pulled into the station and climbed off the train. Bobby Finn grabbed her suitcase from the platform by the guard's van. A British Transport Police officer was waiting for her.

"Here's my card," Detective Parker said, writing something on the back. "I'm giving you my mobile number, as well." He handed it to her. "Don't hesitate to phone me if you need anything."

"Thanks for everything," she said.

"Nonsense, I didn't do anything, but they'll be able to help." He nodded at the Transport Police officer. "Take care of her." He offered his hand to Bobby. "Nice meeting you, Mr. Finn."

"Likewise." They shook.

Parker hailed a cab and disappeared into the night.

"Miss?" The officer motioned for her to join him in the police car.

She hesitated.

"Want me to come with you?" Bobby said, slipping her suitcase onto the seat.

"No, no, you've done enough."

"Here's my mobile number, as well." He handed her a card that read: Agent Bobby Finn, The Blackwell Group, with a Seattle address and phone number. "I'm just bumming in Scotland; I've got nothing pressing on my schedule."

"Okay, thanks." She got into the car, panic filling her stomach, but she wasn't sure why.

"Don't keep her too long," Bobby said to the officer. "She's had a rough go of it."

"We'll make it brief," he said.

She shot Bobby one last smile, hoping he didn't read the panic in her eyes.

She felt a kinship with him. She knew intense experiences made a person crave a warped kind of security. And she sensed Bobby Finn wasn't out to hurt her.

"Ah, move over, I'm coming with." He climbed in beside her.

"Excuse me, sir?" the officer said.

"I saw the man, as well. Maybe I can help."

He winked at Grace, and she knew he wasn't coming along to help with the investigation. He was coming to support her. There were good people out there, too, people you could trust.

"So, miss, your attacker stole your backpack and tied you up? Why do you think he'd do that?" the Transport Officer asked, pulling away from the station.

"I have no idea."

"Do you have any personal enemies?"

"None." She'd lived her life as a pleaser, pleasing her father, her stepmom, even Steven.

"And your mother?" the officer said.

"I'm sorry?" A shudder raced across her shoulders.

"Did she have any enemies?"

"My mother's been dead for years."

"I must have misunderstood. Didn't the man who attacked you make reference to your mother?"

"Yes, but Detective Parker and Mr. Finn thought it was a case of mistaken identity." She glanced at Bobby, who narrowed his eyes at the officer.

"Did he say anything else?" the officer pushed.

Something felt odd about the interrogation in the police car. "He said," she glanced at Bobby, "he said it can be dangerous for single girls traveling in Scotland."

"He said that?" Bobby said. "You didn't mention it before."

"You're on holiday. I didn't want to involve you in all this."

Bobby glared at the back of the officer's head. "Are we nearly there?"

What, was he in that big of a hurry to get away from her, just because she didn't tell him everything the mugger had said?

Sure, of course. She'd attracted another controller into her life, a stranger who thought she owed him every last detail of her attack, probably so he could save her.

Grace didn't want to be saved or protected or smothered. She wanted a life where she could make her own decisions and plan her own future.

But first she had to resolve the past.

"What did you have in your backpack?" the officer asked. "Anything valuable?"

"My wallet, a camera, makeup, a book, things like that."

"A mobile phone?"

"No, I've got my phone with me."

"If you're going to do the complete interview in the car, we'll skip the trip to the station and you can drop us at a hotel," Bobby said.

"I'm just trying to get the details while it's fresh in the girl's mind."

The officer didn't ask any more questions, and she wondered what had happened between the two men. Grace studied Bobby, who stared at the back of the guy's head.

He was angry. Why? It's not like he was the one who was assaulted and had his belongings stolen. He was angry because she hadn't taken him into her confidence, because she hadn't given him control of her situation?

The officer's cell phone rang and he answered it. "I'm with the girl and her friend. Yes… I understand. We'll be there momentarily." He turned the car around and glanced into the rearview mirror. "Apparently there's been a miscommunication," he explained to Grace and Bobby. "They're waiting back at Waverly Station. I apologize."

Grace just wanted some food and a hot bath.

"Where are you from, mate?" Bobby asked him. "Your accent sounds familiar."

The officer didn't answer. Bobby shook his head and glanced out the car window. Grace wondered what was going on between them.

A few minutes later they pulled up to the station and Bobby got out, grabbing her suitcase.

"They're waiting for you inside," the officer said.

She and Bobby went into the station. She glanced around, expecting someone to greet them. There were few people left at the station at this time of night.

Bobby motioned for her to sit on a bench and he sat beside her. "I'm sure they'll find us."

A few minutes passed, and Grace fantasized about finally climbing into a soft bed after this mess of a day.

"It will be over soon," Bobby said, as if he'd read her thoughts.

A man dressed in a British Transport Police uniform walked in their direction.

"Excuse me," Bobby said. "We're here to make a report about a mugging." The man seemed puzzled. "The mugging on the rail from London?"

"Oh, yes, I thought... Never mind. I can help you. I'm Officer Markham." He shook hands with each of them. "Right this way."

He led them down a long hallway into an interview room. "We'll get the details as quickly as possible so you can be on your way."

"The officer who picked us up got plenty of details," Bobby said.

"The officer who picked you up?"

"I didn't catch his name."

"Odd," he said, and motioned for them to sit at a table across from him.

"So, you are Mr. Fairmont?" the officer asked Bobby.

Grace nearly choked at that one. She'd never fall for a man like Bobby Finn, a self-proclaimed troublemaker turned private detective. Although he was charming, she recognized his need to dominate and control.

Grace needed a man who would trust her to take care of herself, a man she could trust, as well. She'd been fooled by her share of boyfriends, lured into romance with false promises.

Trust was key with Grace. And respect.

Although he'd been kind to her, she suspected Bobby Finn was an expert at tempting women into his bed. Not much respect in that.

"I'm just a friend," he clarified. "Bobby Finn."

"And Mr. Finn, you're traveling with Miss Fairmont?"

"We met on the train."

"And you've accompanied her here? What a gentleman."

"Thank you, sir."

Markham narrowed his eyes at Bobby as if trying

to make out his character. "I'd like some basics from you, Mr. Finn, then I'll interview Miss Fairmont." He pulled out a pen and wrote something across a pad of white paper.

Grace sensed that Bobby was uncomfortable, but she couldn't figure out why.

Markham asked questions about home addresses, employment and the reason for Bobby's trip to Scotland. She noticed Bobby fisted his right hand in his lap. Maybe, as doctors make terrible patients, former Scotland Yard detectives make uncomfortable interviewees.

Or maybe he was hiding something.

She was being completely paranoid. Sure she was, she was tired, hungry and still rattled.

The officer moved on to Grace. She answered the questions about her life and recalled what she could about the attack.

A knock interrupted them. The door opened and a second officer walked in holding her backpack.

"You found it!" She shot to her feet and he handed it to her.

"Someone from the train turned it in," the officer explained.

"Excellent," Officer Markham said.

"Not excellent," Bobby argued. "Why did he attack her if he didn't want her pack?"

"Money? Check inside, miss," Markham said.

She dug though her things, makeup case, books

and emergency underwear in case her luggage had been lost. "He took my wallet, but nothing else. The rest of it's here, even the pepper spray. A lot of good that did me," she muttered.

Relief settled low. She could put this incident behind her and move on with her trip. That is, after she notified the credit card companies.

Bobby's cell phone rang. "Will you excuse me?"

"Of course, we're nearly done," Officer Markham said.

Bobby touched her shoulder for support and left the room.

"So, miss? You didn't know Mr. Finn before today?" Markham jotted something down.

"No, why?"

He leveled her with a serious expression. "How much do you know about Bobby Finn?"

BOBBY WENT OUTSIDE to get better reception on his mobile.

"Finn," he answered.

"It's Eddie."

"That was fast."

"Fast is my middle name. Listen, this is one complicated family.

"The mother left. Poof, disappeared one day. Then, about five years later, there's a death notice for Mary Logan, that was her last name. Died in a terrorist bombing in London. Body was messed up. Closed-casket service."

Abandoned by her mother. He glanced toward the station. Bobby knew what that felt like.

"Oh, and this is weirdo stuff," Eddie continued. "The boyfriend, Steven Hunter? I can't find much on him. What's that about, anyway?"

"I'm not sure. But I'm beginning to think the assault on the train was not a coincidence. The bastard said Grace couldn't run away like her mother. That's too close to the truth. Is Max around?"

"Just left with Cassie. Date night."

Good for him, Bobby thought. Max deserved a night out with the woman he loved.

"I'll check back tomorrow," Bobby said. "Fill Max in. He should know what's going on."

"Aye-aye, captain."

Bobby shook his head. "Good night."

Eddie was a character to be sure, and a gifted computer expert. Bobby shoved his mobile into his jacket pocket, puzzling over this new information.

Grace had made it sound as if the mother had died when she was a child. Did she even know the truth—that her mother had disappeared five years before her death? And did the father have anything to do with it?

It amazed Bobby how families could lie so easily.

Da's gone off on a sea journey and wun be back till next year.

You're just stayin' with Uncle Thomas until school lets out. Schools are better in London.

Lies, lies and more lies.

Feeling his life was completely out of control, Bobby had reached out to his aunt and uncle who had nothing to give their precocious nephew.

Feeling unloved, Bobby had reacted the only way an eleven-year-old boy could: he found another family—a local gang.

Those were dark days. Then came Max Templeton, who'd challenged Bobby out of his anger and away from his criminal career.

Max had saved his life, and Bobby would do anything to return the favor.

Which right now meant protecting Miss Grace Fairmont, a woman who was turning out to be her very own mystery. She'd been attacked at random and happened to be dating a man with no past?

He went back into the station to the interview room. He pushed open the door. Grace was gone.

"Where is she?" Bobby asked.

"One of my officers gave her a lift."

"What? To where?"

"She'd made a reservation at a bed and breakfast for the night, paid in full so the missing credit cards are not an issue."

"But…" Bobby glanced out the door, confused and frustrated.

"But what, Mr. Finn?"

"I need to find her."

"She doesn't want to be found. She wants to be left alone."

Bobby stared at him.

"Yes, even from you."

"Bloody hell." He turned and raced out of the station.

Searching the street left, then right, he panicked. He rang Eddie.

"Hey, long time no talk," the computer genius quipped.

"Grace Fairmont's credit cards: find the numbers, trace them. I need to find out where she's staying tonight."

"What, you lost her already? I thought—"

"Just do it, please."

Bobby paced the sidewalk. Blast, if she was hurt again while out of his company—

No, he wouldn't let it happen. He'd only been gone minutes when she'd sneaked out of the station.

Sneaked away. Was she scared of him? Why? What had the Transport Police officer said to make her leave without even saying goodbye?

Now he sounded like a twit. He was a stranger who had offered comfort on a train, nothing more. He didn't deserve another thank-you or goodbye.

"Got it," Eddie said. "The Guest House of Edinburgh at 8 Newington Road."

"Thanks." Bobby clicked off his mobile and hailed a cab.

Instinct told him this wasn't a routine mugging, and this was anything but a routine American woman.

Now, if he could only get to her in time.

HE LIT a fag and glanced across the street at the dark-haired stranger in the leather jacket. This could be a problem.

The man named Bobby Finn climbed into a cab and took off, probably in search of the girl. Why? Who was *he* working for?

He stepped into the phone box and called in. "Eleven o'clock check-in. She's safe in Edinburgh for the time being."

"What does she know?"

"Can't be sure. She had company so I couldn't ask too many questions."

"Intel indicated she'd be traveling alone."

"She made a friend on the train. A man named Bobby Finn. Must be a cop, or former cop. He made me."

Silence.

"No," he clarified. "He doesn't know who I am but he suspected something."

"And the girl? Where is she now?"

"On her way to the inn."

"Did you identify her attacker?"

"Not yet. I'm worried about her new friend. He could complicate things."

"We'll have to take care of him."

"Yes."

"Set him up. Be creative."

"And if he's a cop?"

"All that matters is the girl and finding out what she knows."

"And if she knows nothing?"

"Unfortunate for her. If she doesn't know anything, she's as good as dead."

Chapter Four

Grace sat on her bed, paging through the worn leather diary. As she traced her fingers across the faded pages, she struggled to absorb her mother's thoughts and feelings.

> *An inquisitive little girl, Grace reaches for everything, especially my gold locket. I will give it to her one day, when she's all grown up.*

Grace squeezed the locket in her hand. She could no longer wear it around her neck, thanks to the jerk who'd broken the clasp when he'd ripped it off.

The image of Bobby Finn's soft brown eyes taunted her. She should have said something before leaving, but the officer had a point: she knew nothing about Bobby. He could be a part of the attack on the train.

No, she didn't believe that. She'd left him behind because she felt herself relying on him, appreciating his steady hand and virile strength. She found herself falling into an old pattern of being taken care of by a man and she didn't like it, especially not with a stranger, for Pete's sake.

Still, he'd been helpful and gracious. She'd do the right thing and call his cell phone in the next day or two, apologize for running off and thank him again for his help. After all, she wasn't rude by nature.

And apparently not cautious, either.

She flipped a page in her mother's diary.

> *She has her father's blond hair and blue eyes. I hope she'll grow up looking more like him than me.*

"Why did you want me to look like Dad?"

Someone knocked on her door. She sat straight and closed the diary, marking her place with her locket chain.

"Yes?"

"Miss Fairmont? You'd mentioned wanting to take a bath? It's available," the innkeeper, Mrs. McCarthy, said through the door.

"That would be great."

"I'll put a note on the door and you can have it for thirty minutes then."

"Thanks."

She slipped on her footies and tied her robe around her waist. Her cell phone rang. The caller ID read Dad and she sighed. Well, she couldn't avoid this forever.

"Hi, Dad," she answered, trying to sound perky.

"Gracie," he said in that dad tone. "You were supposed to call when you'd checked in."

"I just got here."

"Just?"

"Have you spoken to Steven?"

"No, why?"

Odd. She figured Steven would have called her father for reinforcements, to convince her to come home.

"There was an incident on the train. I'm fine but it delayed my getting here."

"What kind of incident?"

"Someone stole my backpack. It's okay, though. They found it. Everything is fine."

"You're trying too hard."

"Dad, really, I'm fine. I'm about to take a bath and the clock's ticking on my thirty minutes so if you wouldn't mind, I'll call you tomorrow."

"You promise you're okay?"

"Promise."

"Gracie—"

"Love you, Dad."

"Love you, too, sweetie."

She hung up. Tension started around the base of her throat, that feeling she used to get when she'd try hanging out with a new friend, only to have Dad call the parents. Then he'd call his friend at the police department to do a background check and make her wait until the family had been approved before she could go over to play.

By the time she got there, playtime had been cut in half and the new friend thought Grace a freak with a bossy dad.

Grace knew he meant well. But after all these years would she ever break free of his micromanaging? Ever become her own woman?

She dug in her backpack and pulled out the pepper spray. Maybe she was being paranoid, but she wasn't going anywhere without it from now on. She hoped she'd never have to use it, but holding it in her hand made her feel safe.

She headed down the hall to the bathroom, closed the door and locked it. Filling the tub, she sat on the toilet seat and dropped lavender bath salts into the water.

When she'd started dating Steven she'd thought it progress that Dad hadn't demanded Steven be fingerprinted and checked against the FBI database before her second date. Working for the government, Dad had connections and friends in all kinds of places.

But he'd seemed to trust her decision to date Steven. Dad's confidence made her feel a bit independent, like a mature, grown woman who could make her own choices and take care of herself.

For the most part Steven supported that concept, but every once in a while he'd slip, and it seemed that he was falling into the overprotective role, as well.

Was that because women are attracted to men like their fathers? Had she unwittingly attracted another controlling man into her life?

God, she hoped not. But here, thousands of miles and an ocean away, things looked a bit clearer than they did back home in Illinois. Things seemed a bit clearer since she'd had time to breathe and think without the pressures of school, lesson plans and paper-grading.

Now, if she could recover from the trauma of being attacked on the train she'd actually relax and enjoy this trip.

A trip designed to help her find peace.

She took off her clothes and slipped into the water, letting it warm her skin. She turned off the faucet and leaned back, her arms resting on the rim of the tub.

It felt heavenly, the quiet, the solitude.

After Dad had married Andrea and had two more children, life had been anything but quiet. Grace had wanted to please her new mother, maybe even find love there. Andrea did love Grace, but not the same way a biological mother would love her child. Grace was convinced of this.

She slid down, letting her shoulders rest deeper in the water. It had been Dad who had bathed her as a little girl, fed her and read to her at night.

Dad. He'd always seemed sad growing up, which is why Grace tried so hard to please him, not disobey his wishes. But at what cost? She was now in her twenties and still felt that tug to please him instead of pursuing her own dreams. Sure, she loved teaching science, but a part of her yearned for something more, something exciting.

"Girl, getting away has really mixed you up," she muttered.

Exciting? Grace was the definition of predictability. She didn't need or want anything outside that safe circle.

Or did she?

The lights went out and she was plunged into complete darkness. She sat up and reached for the pepper spray. Gripping it in her hand she heard the doorknob rattle.

Her heart slammed against her chest. Naked, wet and alone.

Vulnerable.

A flash of memory sparked panic.

Lights out. A stranger's presence. Grace was only five.

But she wasn't five now.

"Who's there?" she called.

Pepper spray in hand, she got out of the tub and fumbled in the dark, drying off the best she could. It wasn't pitch-black, thanks to the streetlight outside.

"Miss Fairmont?" the innkeeper called through the door. "We've had a power outage. I'm terribly sorry. Are you okay?"

"Fine, thanks."

She managed to get her robe on and tie the sash, her fingers trembling from the cold. Or was it fear?

"I've put a lantern in the hallway so you can find your way back to your room."

"Thank you."

Grace heard the floorboards squeak as the woman went back downstairs.

"It's okay. Breathe," she ordered herself. With arms straight out and a finger on the pepper spray, she opened the door. She grabbed the lantern and went to her room, shaking off the sensation that someone was behind her, too close, within reach.

She'd always been scared of the dark. Ever since the lights had gone out when she was five and had waited for Dad to return with the flashlight. She could have sworn someone was there, with her in the bathroom.

Just like she felt someone was behind her now.

She spun around pointing the pepper spray at her imaginary stalker. The short hallway was empty.

"Get a grip," she muttered.

She turned and opened the door to her room.

"Grace," a deep voice said from the corner.

She screamed and fired off the pepper spray.

"Bloody Christ," a man said, coughed and collapsed to the floor. "Grace, don't. It's Bobby."

Bobby struggled to breathe, his eyes burning, his chest tightening as if someone was squeezing the air out of his lungs.

"How did you find me?" she cried.

"I'll explain." Cough. Cough. "I have to...talk to you."

He wheezed, struggling to breathe. Blast, if she called the police on him he'd be taken away for questioning and she'd be vulnerable again.

"What's all this?" Mrs. McCarthy said, rushing to Grace's room.

"Grace, please," he said.

"Call the police," she said to the innkeeper.

The woman dashed off.

"You have to—" Cough. "Listen."

"The detective was right. You were part of the attack on the train, weren't you?"

She got down in his face, as he struggled to breathe.

"Tell me what you want," she demanded, then she shoved that bloody pepper spray at him again.

He lost it and grabbed her wrist away from his face. Although he couldn't focus his watering eyes, he could feel the warmth of her breath on his skin.

"I'm not the enemy," he rasped.

He snatched the spray canister from her hand, tossed it aside and stood, knocking something off a dressing table. He leaned against the wall wishing the effects of the spray would pass, so he could explain why he was here.

And how would that conversation go, mate? I'm the babysitter hired by your daddy?

"What do you want?" she said.

His eyes burned as if they were on fire. "I need cold water." He stumbled out of her room and down the hall to the toilet.

He bent over the sink and turned on the cold water, cupping his hands. He splashed his eyes three, four times. Bugger, too many coincidences: the assault, the imposter officer who drove them around tonight and now the lights going out.

The bathroom door closed with a click. Grace stood there holding the damn pepper spray.

"Don't do that again," he said. "Please."

"Then tell me what this is really about."

"It's about your safety."

"And you care why?"

"It's my job."

"As a private detective?"

"Yes."

He splashed more water on his face.

"Who hired you?"

Now what? If he told her she'd be furious and if he didn't tell her she'd demand the police take him away.

Bugger, she'd probably insist they lock him up anyway.

"Your father hired me," he admitted.

"How could he?"

"Simple. He rang my boss, asked for help protecting his little girl, and I'm practically blinded for my trouble." He pressed a cool washcloth to his eyes.

"How much is he paying you?" she said.

"I'm sorry?"

"I'll double it if you leave me alone."

He slowly lowered the washcloth and looked at her through the mirror. Was she that offended by his presence?

Sure she was. Grace was about dignity and class; Bobby came from street rubbish.

No matter. He had a job to do.

"I'm not leaving you alone," he said. "This job is important to me and I'd rather you not muck it up because you're on an independent streak."

"You make it sound so frivolous."

"Isn't it?"

"You wouldn't understand."

"I understand this." He turned and squared off at her. "You've got a father who wants you safe. He knows you have a sweet look about you that makes you a target and he cares enough to hire someone to watch after you. You're lucky you've got someone who cares so much."

"I'm twenty-six, dammit, I don't want a bodyguard."

"Maybe it's not about what you want. Do this for your father. Give him peace of mind."

And help me keep my job. He didn't say it. He

knew she thought him the enemy. She couldn't care less about Bobby's job, his future.

She wrapped her arms around her midsection. "It always has been about him. I was doing this for me."

"No one's stopping you." He sighed and placed his hands to his hips. "Look, everyone can get what they want. You can have your holiday; your father can have peace of mind and I can keep my job."

Grace had imagined the compassion in his eyes, earlier, the tenderness. It wasn't real.

"This was all about your job," she said in a flat tone.

"It's my life. I don't have family like you."

"Aren't you lucky."

"Miss Fairmont?" a man called through the door. "This is the police."

She pressed the back of her head against the door and studied Bobby Finn. He was a charmer to be sure, convincing her that he cared about her safety.

"Please, Grace," Bobby said, his eyes still red and watering. "If they take me in I can't protect you."

"From what? There's nothing to protect me from. I got mugged. It's over."

"I couldn't stand it if anything else happened to you."

"Why, because they'd dock your salary?"

He stared at her, but didn't answer.

"Miss Fairmont?" the officer called again.

She opened the door. "I'm sorry, but there's been a misunderstanding. It was dark and I couldn't see who it was."

"Are you saying you know this man?"

She glanced over her shoulder. "Yes, he's a friend. He wanted to surprise me."

"Scared the wits out of me," Mrs. McCarthy said.

"Please, come into the hall, miss," the officer said. She followed him and shut the bathroom door.

"You're sure you're all right?" he asked.

"I'm fine." *Just angry as hell.*

"But he broke into your room," Mrs. McCarthy said.

"My fault, actually," she lied. "I left the door unlocked. It's okay. He was trying to surprise me."

"Looks like he got the surprise with pepper spray in the face." He glanced at the cylinder in her hand.

"Yeah, well." She slipped it into her robe pocket.

"Since all's well then." The officer nodded and started down the stairs. Grace heard Mrs. McCarthy offer him tea for his trouble.

Grace glanced at the bathroom door. Great, just what she didn't want on this trip: a shadow. Wasn't that part of the purpose? To prove she could live her own life independently of men like her father?

She opened the door to find Bobby coughing and splashing water on his face. Regret settled across her shoulders. She did feel bad that she'd sprayed the very man who'd given her comfort on the train.

Because it was his job.

"Here's the deal," she said.

He turned and blinked repeatedly.

"I need my space. Lots of it. I have things to do on this trip. Personal things."

"I understand."

She sighed. "If I'd wanted company I would have invited Steven."

"Of course," he said, his face set like stone.

"Fine, I'll see you in the morning." She opened the door and started down the hall. "I'll be stopping by the American Express office to pick up a new credit card. The rest will take a few days to get here, so I'll probably do the sights." She opened the door to her room. "Good night."

Bobby glanced down the hall. She had a corner room, which was good. He'd curl up against the wall and sit outside her door. Might be overkill, then again, might not be.

He still wasn't sure what to make of this assignment.

Although, he was getting a clearer picture of Miss Grace Fairmont. She was tougher than he'd originally thought, determined as hell, and a bit self-centered. All she could think about were her own needs, taking this trip regardless of her father's worry.

And he should be worried. Bobby wasn't fibbing when he'd said she had a look about her that drew unsavory characters. Sweet, innocent and trusting. That's what Miss Fairmont looked like on the outside.

But then people weren't always what they seemed if Bobby's last case was any indication.

If his own family was any indication.

Mum had always seemed so loving.

Loving parents don't abandon their children.

"Ah, that's what happens when you come home, Bobby," he muttered.

Home? He sat on the hardwood floor and studied the knickknacks on the table in the hallway. This is what a real home looked like: warm and cozy.

He'd never lived in any home like this. No, his first home was filled with sadness, and his second home with judgment and disappointment.

In Bobby.

He wouldn't disappoint Max Templeton. He didn't care what hoops she made him jump through; he'd do whatever it took to stay close to Grace Fairmont and complete his assignment.

Crossing his legs at the ankles, he leaned against the wall. He took a deep breath, inhaling the scent of lavender, realizing it was Grace's scent that hovered in the hallway outside her door.

It was a good thing he was methodical when it came to women. He always called the shots, deciding when a relationship would start and how long it would last. Never more than a few months, of course. He wasn't a fool. He wouldn't completely give his heart, knowing that in the end the woman would abandon him for a smarter chap, a better provider.

No, you couldn't count on a woman for anything but great sex. Most of the time, anyway.

He glanced at Grace's door. He'd bet she was a wild one between the sheets, the outwardly reserved ones usually were. Not that he'd ever know firsthand. Becoming intimate with this woman was dangerous on so many levels.

Grace Fairmont was the type you wanted to take care of and protect. The most dangerous kind. They drew you in and stole your heart while you were busy buying them flowers or tickets to Elton John concerts.

SMACK! Just like *that* you'd be knocked on your bum and wouldn't even know what hit you.

Because she was smarter than you.

Because she stole your heart and now you were half a man.

Not that he'd ever lost his heart completely. He'd come close twice, and both times he'd managed to rip himself out of the fire before he got burned too badly.

It was good experience to recognize the dangerous ones.

And Grace Fairmont was dangerous as hell.

SHE PACED her small room, did the deep-breathing technique Steven had taught her and opened her cell phone to call Dad.

Bobby's words taunted her. *You're lucky you've got someone who cares so much.*

Is that what you called it? Luck?

Grace called it a curse, especially as she'd gotten older and Dad had never loosened up. She was an adult woman. When was he going to get that through his head?

She hit the speed-dial number and it rang.

"Hello?" he answered.

"Dad?"

"What's wrong?"

"Your bodyguard."

Silence.

"Dad, I'm twenty-six. You can't do stuff like this."

"How did you find out?"

"He told me."

"Out of the blue a complete stranger walks up to you and announces he's your bodyguard?"

"No, it's complicated."

"It started on the train, didn't it? When you had your little incident?"

"Yes, that's how we met. Then he showed up in my room and now I want him out of my life."

"Why was he in your room?"

"I didn't ask. I got him with pepper spray."

"You were prepared. Good girl."

"I don't feel very good. You know what a guy looks like after he's been sprayed?"

"I can imagine."

Grace didn't have to. The image of Bobby's bloodshot eyes and vulnerable position on the floor haunted her. She hated inflicting that kind of pain, especially to someone who'd helped her only hours earlier.

Helped her because he was paid to help her.

"I want to do this alone, Dad. I want to tour Scotland and learn about my mother. On my own."

"Let him follow you, Grace. You won't even know he's there."

She heard Bobby cough outside her door.

"Dad, I'm not a little girl anymore. It's time you let go."

Silence.

"Dad?"

"I will, honey. I promise. As soon as you return from your trip I'll give you your space."

"I need it now."

"No."

"No? Okay, now I have to play Mission Impossible and escape from my bodyguard?"

"Grace, please don't do that. For my peace of mind please let him do his job. I…" He hesitated. "I have my reasons."

"Dad, I love you but you've got to stop—"

"I can't, Gracie. Not while you're out of the country. There are things you don't know." He hesitated. "Things about your mother."

Chapter Five

Her heart beat a little faster. "What kind of things?" she asked.

"This isn't something you talk to your daughter about over the phone, Grace."

Oh, God, what was it?

"Dad, you're freaking me out here."

"Your mother was and will continue to be a mystery to me in many ways. We loved each other, but she had her secrets."

Grace sat on the bed and thought about Steven, and how she kept a part of herself hidden from him, not entirely sure why.

"What do Mom's secrets have to do with me?"

"She ran with a wild group back in the U.K.," he said. "I'm not sure what they were into, but when I'd ask her about her life there she'd withdraw and look so terribly sad. After a few months I stopped asking. I'm afraid it might have been illegal and I wouldn't want anything to happen to you because of things your mother did."

"Wait a second, you always made her out to be this loving, compassionate mother who'd do anything for her child."

"She loved you so very much."

Grace couldn't remember that love thanks to a drunk driver hitting mom's car head-on. Hell, if it wasn't for the photo in Grace's locket she wouldn't know what her mother looked like—and now that was gone.

"What do you think she was into, exactly?" she said.

"I have no idea. But it was ugly. She may have even spent some time in jail."

"Jail... Is that why you didn't want me to take this trip? Because you were afraid I'd find out the truth?"

"There's only one truth, Gracie. Your mother loved you. Whoever she was ten years before she gave birth to you, she was no longer that person."

That *really* didn't sound good.

"Do you know why she was in prison?"

"I don't even know for sure she was in prison. She wouldn't talk about her past or her family. But the way she acted in public, suspicious, like she was on the alert all the time, made me wonder."

"I wish you had told me this before."

"I know, honey. I'm sorry. I didn't want you to think ill of your mom."

Grace wasn't sure what this trip would reveal, but whether good or bad, she was determined to find some kind of resolution. Even if it meant she'd discover the dark side of her supposedly loving mother.

No, not supposedly. It didn't matter what her mom had been into, because she *was* a loving mother. Her diary proved it with every word about her baby girl, Gracie.

"Can we compromise?" he said.

"How?"

"You finish out this trip with the bodyguard close by and I'll work on easing up when you get home. Please, Gracie, just this one last time."

She sighed. It started to make sense: Dad's over-protectiveness and micromanaging. He'd been left alone to raise a baby girl. A big responsibility when you shared it with someone and even bigger when you were doing it on your own. Isn't that what she'd learned from the parents of middle-schoolers? The single parents struggled so hard to give their children everything they needed, fighting time constraints and just plain exhaustion from burning the candle at both ends.

She thought about the time Dad had rushed her to the hospital after she'd broken her wrist, the times he sat up with her because of night terrors. She used to dream of monsters hiding in the shadows of her room; she used to hear someone breathing.

Dad had done so much for her, on his own. And he was asking this one simple thing.

"Okay," she said. "I'll keep the bodyguard."

"Thank you, Gracie." He sounded tired, weary.

"I'll even try not to blast him with pepper spray again," she joked.

"That's a good girl."

She smiled. She'd be fifty and he'd still be calling her a good girl.

"What's on the agenda for tomorrow?" he asked.

"The Royal Mile. Edinburgh Castle and Holyrood, I think." She thought about her chat with Bobby on the train. "I heard it's fantastic."

"I thought you were heading up north right away."

"I have to wait for replacement credit cards. I can pick up a new Am Ex card, but I have to hang around for the others."

"You should have brought traveler's checks."

"Thanks, yeah, I've figured that out."

"I'm sorry, of course you have. I'm doing it again. Okay, sweetheart. You have a wonderful time. Check in once in a while, okay?"

"I will, Dad, promise."

"Love you."

"Love you back. 'Bye."

She pressed the End button and placed the phone on her nightstand. Mom's diary caught her eye. Would Grace find hidden meanings there? Something to reveal her mother's secrets, her dark past?

"Oh, stop. Dad's overreacting," she muttered.

True, but he overreacted because he cared. She could hardly fault him for loving her so much.

For eight years Dad had done so many things for her without help from a wife. He'd done pretty darn well for a single father.

She had to respect him for that. And now that she knew the truth about Mom, Grace understood why this trip in particular made Dad nervous. She wished he'd spoken with her in person instead of hiding the truth.

Was he worried that she couldn't handle it? That she'd idolized her mother so much the truth would destroy Grace?

No, regardless of what her father thought, Grace knew she was stronger than that, tougher. She didn't need to be protected and she surely didn't need a bodyguard.

Yet she was stuck with the handsome Bobby Finn.

She opened the door and there in the corner of the hallway sat her bodyguard.

"You can't sleep out here," she whispered.

"Sure I can. Unless they call the police back."

He sniffed and rubbed his eyes.

Guilt snagged her conscience.

She went back into her room and grabbed a spare pillow and blanket.

"I spoke with Dad." She tossed the pillow and blanket at him. "You've still got a job."

"Lovely," he said with a forced smile.

"Look, I'm sorry about the pepper spray."

"I'm not. It means you're on the ball this time."

This time, right, not like when she'd been attacked on the train. The stairs creaked, and Grace took a step toward her room. Bobby stood as if ready for a confrontation.

Mrs. McCarthy stepped into the hallway and glanced at Bobby and then Grace. "What's this?"

"He's…we're…" What should she say? If she admitted Bobby was her bodyguard it would surely alarm the woman. "We're having an argument," Grace blurted out.

"Well, I'm sorry, but your friend is going to have to leave. He can't sleep on the floor and we don't have any rooms available tonight."

Bobby looked so completely disheartened.

"Come on now," the innkeeper said. "You'd best be off. I think the Greystone Inn down the block has a few single rooms open." She motioned with her hand.

Bobby didn't move. He was going to get them both kicked out of the inn.

"No, it's okay," Grace said. "He can stay in my room." She glanced at Mrs. McCarthy. "Can't he?"

"I'll have to charge you an extra ten pounds."

"Of course." Grace glanced at Bobby, who clutched the pillow and blanket, but hadn't moved.

"Well?" Mrs. McCarthy prompted.

Bobby grudgingly walked toward Grace and hesitated as he passed her. His eyes were dark and intense as if he was furious, and for a split second she thought better of inviting him in to spend the night.

He disappeared into her room.

"Thank you so much," she said to Mrs. McCarthy. "I'm not used to so much excitement."

"I'm sorry."

"You'll keep it quiet up here?"

"Yes, ma'am."

What, did she think they were lovers?

With pursed lips the woman nodded and turned to go downstairs. She wasn't happy. Well, neither was Grace. She'd wanted solitude and peace on this trip. Instead, she was stuck with a sexy stranger as her shadow.

She went into her room and shut the door. Bobby stood by the window, peeking through the sheers. "I'll wait a few hours and go back in the hallway."

"Oh, okay." She climbed into bed and turned off the bedside light. "Good night."

He didn't respond.

She lay there, eyes partially closed, watching his silhouette as he stood guard at the window. Strangely enough, she felt safer with him here.

Resentment took hold. She wanted to stand on her own, without her father or a bodyguard or Steven holding her hand.

"What happened?" Bobby said.

She opened her eyes. "What do you mean?"

"What made you ask me into your room?"

"My dad explained why he's worried about me. I agreed to keep you around."

"Keep me around? Like a stray puppy?" He laughed.

"I didn't mean it like that."

"It's okay. I'm used to it."

A few more minutes passed. She suddenly wished she knew more about this man's personal life. No, it was better not to know. There was something about Bobby that excited and intrigued her.

"I have to admit this is a first," he said.

"What?"

"Spending the night with a woman, but not in her bed."

Grace clutched the down comforter tighter to her chest. She'd sensed he was one of those guys, the kind that enjoyed sexual affairs but never engaged in love. She'd dated a few men like that. Thank goodness she'd found Steven.

She sighed. Solid, predictable Steven. Dad had been so relieved when she'd found him, especially after her wild teenage years.

She was lucky that Steven had come into her life, moved into her apartment complex and soon afterward, introduced himself. That had been two years ago. She wondered why she'd put him off for so long, discouraged him from making his official proposal.

"Are you married?" she asked Bobby.

"You've had a rough day," he said. "Get some sleep."

Obviously she'd hit a sore spot. Well, if she was going to spend the next two weeks in his company, she didn't want it to be awkward.

"Sorry," she said.

"For what?"

She propped herself up and studied his silhouette as he continued to stare out the window. "I didn't mean to pry."

"Don't let it happen again."

She heard humor in his voice and struggled to read his expression in the dark.

"It's fine. Go to sleep," he said.

She lay back down and pulled the comforter up to her shoulders. "Good night."

"Sweet dreams."

Her last conscious thought was how odd those words sounded coming from Bobby Finn's mouth.

THE NEXT DAY, Bobby followed Grace to the American Express office where she got a replacement card. Apparently she'd need it.

She spent the morning buying gifts for family and friends back home. Bobby had never intentionally gone shopping with a woman. He considered it torture.

Yet with Grace it wasn't so bad. She was genuinely enthusiastic about every purchase as if she'd struck gold. It was hard to stay cross with that kind of enthusiasm smiling back at you.

"Look at this wool scarf," she said. "It'll be perfect for Dad, and the girls, they'll love the Scotland flag patches. They'll put them on their denim jackets and they'll feel so cool."

She shoved them back into her bag and shrugged, grinning from ear to ear.

She wore her hair straight today, framing her round face and full lips. She looked enticing, like a female he'd proposition.

"What? You think I should have gotten Dad a different plaid?"

"It's fine." He recovered, snapping his gaze from hers. Bugger, she'd noticed he'd drifted into lust. *Not good, mate.* "You know whose pattern that is?" he said.

"Who?" She started walking and he kept pace beside her.

"The Black Watch."

"Sounds sinister."

"On the contrary, it's an infantry battalion of the Royal Regiment of Scotland. This country has had quite the history, always fighting for independence, always fighting to establish its own identity."

"I can relate."

"Can you?" he teased. "Well, at least no blood's been shed over your independence."

"Not yet, anyway." She smiled at him and he wondered if the threat was aimed at Bobby or at her father.

"Hey, what about you? You haven't bought anything today," she said.

"Shopping isn't my favorite pastime, although now that you mention it, I could use a few pairs of trousers and shirts. I didn't have time to pack before I got on the train."

"Okay, great. I used to love helping Dad shop for clothes, especially when he started dating."

"You didn't feel threatened by that? The other women?"

"He didn't date all that many and besides, I wanted a mother so badly. For a long time I thought it was my fault I didn't have one."

He hesitated and touched her jacket. "Your fault?"

"Yeah, y'know, if he didn't have me around he would have found a wife faster, stuff like that. You think weird stuff when you're a kid."

Or not so weird. Bobby had cried so hard when his mum left him with Uncle Thomas. She'd said he needed a male role model, but Bobby knew it was something else. He'd failed. Miserably, and she couldn't stand having him around.

"Hey, I'm over it," she said. She studied him with worry in her eyes. "You know, before this trip is over you're going to have to tell me what puts that look on your face."

"What look?"

"You go like this." She clenched her jaw and narrowed her eyes.

"I do not look like that."

"Uh, yeah, you really do."

Blast, he was that transparent?

"Help me pick out some clothes," he said, picking up the pace.

"My pleasure."

Bloody marvelous, now he was her pet project. She'd probably dress him in fancy trousers, a tailored shirt and stuffy tie.

"Why is it so important to you?" she said.

"What, clothes?"

"Your job?"

"It's my life's work."

"Following American girls around?"

"Catching bad guys, putting them away where they can't hurt anyone. This—" he motioned to the space between them "—is a temporary diversion."

A pleasant diversion.

She glanced away and he thought he might have hurt her feelings. How could that be? He didn't say anything out of order.

Yet Bobby, the master of flirtation, put his foot in it on more than one occasion with this girl.

"I'll bet you can get something in here." She steered him into a shop selling wool sweaters, tartan trousers and colorful souvenirs. "Look at all this stuff," she said, her eyes wide as they scanned the wares.

"What's your plaid?" she said.

"I don't have one."

He didn't have a plaid; didn't have a homeland, although he was born in Ireland, he'd been shipped off to England for the better part of his life.

"Everyone's got a plaid, right?" she said.

He shook his head. "Americans."

"I'll pick one out for you. Something that complements your eyes."

"I wear black," he said, sounding like a child. "Black trousers, black jacket."

"Okay, then we'll find you a shirt. Black plaid, perhaps?" She winked.

He stood behind her as she sifted through the rack of clothes. Instincts always on alert, he scanned the tourists filling the shop, paying attention to any oddities or anyone unusually interested in Grace.

Could the attack on the train and the power outage at the inn be simple coincidences? Possibly. He hoped so. He didn't like the thought that this girl on holiday was at risk.

"This one," she said, pulling a plaid shirt from the rack. "Large, right?"

"It's bloody purple," he said.

"It's maroon and it will look great. Hold it for me." She handed it to him and glanced behind him. Her brows furrowed.

He turned to see what she was looking at.

People milled about picking through the scarves and hats on sale. He looked back at her.

"I'm seeing things," she said.

"What things?"

"My boyfriend. I swear I just saw him walk out the front door. They say everyone's got a double. That must have been him." She turned back to the rack of shirts.

Bobby glanced out the front window of the store. He wished he knew what the bloke looked like. He made a mental note to have Eddie send him a photograph of the boyfriend.

She turned and handed him another shirt.

"No, absolutely not," Bobby said. "I may be color blind, but I know pink when I see it."

"Just kidding." She shot him that silly smile of hers and put it back.

When she smiled he wanted to touch her cheek, trace his thumb across her soft skin.

He took a slight step back. He really didn't need to fall into lust with this girl. She was classy, had a boyfriend, led an uncomplicated life.

Unlike Bobby.

Bobby was broken in more ways than he could count, and he'd never be capable of giving true love to a woman. That was just fine with him.

"Okay, try these on and I'll be waiting outside the dressing room," she said.

"Right outside?"

"Of course, I wouldn't want to miss the fashion show."

With her hand to his back she pushed him to a dressing room. He peeked through the slit between the drape and the wall to make sure she hadn't strayed too far. She was right outside the dressing room.

In record time he changed into the wild plaid trousers and a clashing shirt. Colors to complement his eyes? Rubbish. He looked in the mirror and nearly burst out laughing. He only hoped it had the same effect on Grace.

He flung open the drape. "I may be color blind but—"

She was gone.

"Grace?"

Maybe she was looking for more clashing patterns.

"If you're looking for the blond woman, she ran out the front door," a teenage girl said.

Bobby glanced through the storefront window and spotted Grace outside.

"Grace!" he called after her. He raced through the store, the clerk calling after him.

What on earth was she doing running away? Was it all a ruse? A game to get free of him?

Bobby pushed through tourists and raced into the street, only now aware that he wasn't wearing shoes and had left his wallet in the dressing room in his pants.

Bollocks, where had she gone?

"Grace!" he called down the street.

He thought he saw her blond head through the crowd of tourists and pushed through to get to her.

"Stop! Thief!" someone cried behind him.

"Grace!" he shouted again.

Sirens echoed down the street. God, no, she wasn't hit by a car or injured or—

"I don't think so," a man said, grabbing Bobby's arm. He wrenched free, racing after her, desperate to keep her safe.

Maybe if he had kept Wendy safe Mum wouldn't have sent him away.

For crying out loud, where had that come from?

Something tripped him and suddenly there were three men pinning him to the sidewalk. He heard a woman's cries. His heart clenched with panic.

The sirens wailed. She couldn't be hurt. He'd never forgive himself.

"Get off me." He struggled against his aggressors. He couldn't budge.

The dozen faces standing over him parted and two police officers looked down at him.

One of the officers shook his head in disgust. "All this for a pair of purple trousers?"

Chapter Six

"Hold on a bloody minute, it's a misunderstanding," Bobby protested as the police pulled him to his feet and walked him to the squad car.

He still couldn't believe they'd cuffed him for running off with a pair of ridiculous purple trousers. He hadn't given much thought to dashing into the crowded street wearing the store's gear. He'd been too worried about Grace.

As they shoved him into the back of the police car he fought back his shame. He'd failed at so many things in his life. Why should this be any different?

Bugger, where had she disappeared to and why? Was this shopping lark her clever way of giving him the slip?

"Hey, wait!" a woman cried.

Grace. He turned and looked into her concerned blue eyes.

"Why are you arresting him?" she demanded.

"He stole these trousers right off the rack."

"No, it's a mistake. It's my fault."

"Sorry, miss, we're taking him in."

"My clothes are still in the fitting room," Bobby shouted as the officer shut the door.

Grace said something to the copper, probably asking where they were taking Bobby, then she ran off.

Alone.

And Bobby was stuck in the back of a squad car, helpless and unable to protect her. When he was released he should call Max to have someone else assigned to this case. Eddie maybe. He'd be a lot of fun for Grace and good American company.

"So, you do this often, Finn? Run off in other peoples' trousers?"

Bobby's blood ran cold. "You know my name?"

The cop didn't answer. Bobby glanced out the car window. They headed away from the Royal Mile, away from town.

"Where are we going?" Bobby asked.

"Some place where we can talk."

Not good. Were these blokes truly the police?

"Talk about what?"

"About how we don't appreciate known criminals showing up and mingling with our tourists."

"I wasn't mingling with anyone."

"No, you were just caught stealing. We know all about you, Bobby. Officer Markham at Transport Police pulled your criminal history. We know about the breaking and entering and drug-peddling."

"That's not true." His temper flared.

"Records never lie, mate. We're going to give you a re-education before you decide to hook up with your old friends."

"A thorough background check would also reveal I'd been with Scotland Yard."

"He's got a sense of humour, that one," the driver said to his partner.

"Either that or he's off his trolley."

"I was with the Special Crimes Initiative," Bobby said.

"Definitely off his trolley."

It didn't matter what they did to him, but someone had to watch out for Grace.

"I've been hired to look after the girl," he said. "At least call in and have someone check on her."

"Why, she looked pretty independent to me," the driver said.

"You should have heard her read me the riot act because I was taking her boyfriend into custody. She's got a mouth on her."

"Her father hired me to accompany her on this trip," Bobby explained.

"Now why would he do that?" the driving cop said.

"He didn't tell me why. He just said he was worried about her."

"Ah, she'll be fine. She's meeting us at the station," the other one said.

"She'll be waiting a long time," his partner said. They chuckled.

"Listen to me!" Bobby pounded on the seat between them. "I need to get back to her."

The lead cop turned around and eyed Bobby. "You'll get back when we're done."

THEY PULLED into an old warehouse parking lot.

"In there," the driver cop said. "No one will hear anything."

Adrenaline pounded through Bobby's veins. He was going to be beaten and tortured. Why? Because of his criminal background? No, there was something else going on here.

They parked and the lead cop opened his door. "Out with ya."

Bobby took a deep breath, scooted out and shouldered the guy in the gut. They both went down.

"Christ almighty!" the guy said.

Bobby was pulled off by the second cop, who spun him around and slugged him in the gut. Bobby went down gasping for breath.

"He messed up my uniform," the first cop said, kicking him in the chest.

Bobby rolled away, his ribs aching from the kick.

"Let's get this over with. Hold him."

Bobby was pulled to his feet and held up by one cop while the other slugged him again. Sure, they didn't want to damage his face or anything so obvious.

As he struggled to recover, something pricked his arm. He was tossed to the gravel drive, his head slamming against the rugged stones.

He lay there, dazed, trying to make sense of what was happening. All this for stealing a pair of trousers and a shirt? Bollocks. Even with his record, his criminal background was nothing compared to his years at Scotland Yard, where he'd tried desperately to make up for his sins.

Where he'd met Max Templeton and got a second chance, and a third with the Blackwell Group: finding a serial killer, saving a lost boy, protecting Grace.

Max. Cassie. Grace.

She was vulnerable, too innocent. Too sweet to be involved in anything like this.

Like what? Like violence and torture?

Torture. Failure. Grace. He was failing again.

Couldn't think. Thoughts spinning as if he'd drunk too much ale. A pint. Three pints. How much had he had with Art last night? He couldn't remember. Couldn't remember why he was here on the ground, gravel digging into his cheek.

Suddenly sitting up.

Who hired him? Why was he watching Grace? What about her mother?

That's why Grace was here, in Scotland, yes, that's why she'd come. She wanted to find out about her mum, where she'd lived as a girl.

The past. Leave the past alone. Bobby knew that.

Hadn't spoken to Uncle Thomas since his aunt's funeral. Bastard.

The man on the train. His name? Harry Franklin. Earring, worn trainers, expensive suit. Inspector Parker. Helpful chap. Gave her his card.

His brain fast-forwarded through the last forty-eight hours. He could hardly focus. The fall must have knocked him senseless.

Brains rattled. Would be fine in the morning. They were trying to help him, keep him on the straight and narrow.

Like Max. Max always helped. Had faith in Bobby.

Where was he going next? Up north, where?

Maybe Pitlochry. Mentioned in her diary.

Diary?

Dark leather, with ties. Saw it on her nightstand. Mother's notes to her daughter. Dead mother.

What happened to mother?

Died in a car accident. Died when Grace was a baby. Didn't know her mum.

Where did Mum grow up?

Don't know. Mum was gone, dead. Grace was a baby. Grace…she didn't like having someone follow her, act as her bodyguard.

Not much of a bodyguard, is he? They're calling. Have to report back.

Pulled to his feet. Bobby struggled to get balance.

Must have hit his head when he fell outside the

shop. Probably a concussion. Will take him to a clinic, call the girl. He'll be fine.

In the backseat, spinning, everything spinning.

Thought they were going to torture him. Paranoid chap.

Blur of images, buildings, steel fence. Feeling sick. Close eyes.

Relax, mate. Would be over soon. Would wake up right as rain.

"Grace." He breathed her name.

Save her. Had to help her. Had to…sleep.

GRACE PACED around Bobby's hospital bed. The police believed he'd knocked himself stupid when his head hit the sidewalk. Bull. He was conscious when they drove off. Something else had happened to him. He'd been out for three hours.

If this wasn't a case of brutality, she didn't know what was. He'd obviously been knocked unconscious by the two cops who'd arrested him outside the shop.

Why? It was a misunderstanding. Guilt tore at her stomach. If she hadn't run off, chasing after a ghost who looked like her boyfriend, Bobby wouldn't have run out of the store after her. He wouldn't have been taken away by the cops and wouldn't be lying in a hospital bed.

"Miss Fairmont?" A man wearing a navy suit, crisp white shirt and maroon tie stood in the doorway.

"Yes?" She stepped closer to Bobby and touched his hand in a protective gesture.

"I'm Detective Inspector Owen. I want to apologize for any misunderstanding." He took a few steps into the room.

"No misunderstanding," she said. "Your men abused my friend."

"I'm sorry you think so, miss. I'll look into it."

"You do that."

She stroked the back of Bobby's hand. She and Bobby had the absolute worst luck.

"It's an easy fix," the inspector said.

She glared at him. "Really?"

"We'll drop the theft charges and you don't pursue this line of thinking."

"You mean the one that dictates I notify your superiors about police brutality?"

He glanced at the floor and crossed his arms over his chest. "There's no point in that, miss. If your boyfriend hadn't stolen the clothes none of this would have happened."

"He didn't steal anything. He ran out of the shop because he was worried about me."

"Why's that, miss?"

She shook her head. Bobby seemed to be sleeping so peacefully.

"You're here on holiday then?" the inspector asked.

"Yes."

"I'd hate to hold you up with unnecessary paperwork. I'll give your bloke the benefit of the doubt and you can be on your way."

"Gee, thanks."

"Unless you feel that's unfair."

"It's fine," she said, frustrated, wanting to head north sooner than later.

"Good day, then."

She didn't look up, but sensed the inspector leave the room.

She squeezed Bobby's hand, remembering what the doctor had said. It seemed like a minor concussion, nothing to be alarmed about. Then why was he still asleep?

She sat in the chair and rubbed the back of his hand. He looked so still and broken, nothing like the man who'd protected her on the train or stood watch outside her room at the inn.

He seemed completely drained of energy.

Because of her.

No, she wouldn't take full responsibility. She didn't want him tagging along on this trip. That had been Dad's idea.

"Wendy," Bobby muttered.

Great, now he was dreaming about old girlfriends.

"Bobby? It's me, Grace. Can you hear me?"

He moaned and squeezed the sheets between his fingers.

"Shh. It's okay now," she said.

"No!" He sat up, gasping for air. His eyes were open but not totally focused.

"Bobby, look at me. It's Grace. Do you know who I am?"

"Grace?" His brown eyes widened, he swallowed, then fell back against the bed. "Where am I?"

"At the hospital. You lost consciousness."

"How?"

"They said when you fell and hit your head on the sidewalk, remember? Outside the tartan store?"

He pinned her with his gaze. "You were gone."

"I'm sorry, really, I'm an idiot."

"Where did you go?"

"It's stupid, and now it caused this. I feel like a jerk."

"Where?"

"I saw that guy, the one who looks like Steven, and I thought it was him. He glanced at me through the window and gave me this weird look. I ran outside but lost him in the crowd. You ran after me and forgot to change your pants. The cops came for you and you fell and knocked your head on the cement, which makes no sense because you spoke to me before they took you away."

"What did I say?"

"You said that your pants were still in the fitting room. I got them, and your wallet and went to the station. Then the cops called and said you were being brought to the hospital."

"I fell. Hit my head on the rocks."

"Not rocks, the sidewalk. Do you remember?"

"Not really."

"He's awake?" A doctor came into the room with a clipboard in his hand. "Excellent."

"He doesn't remember things," she said.

"To be expected. There's minor swelling around the brain, nothing serious, but even a slight contusion can cause memory issues. You remember this pretty lass, eh, Bobby?" the doctor said.

Bobby looked at her. "I remember Grace."

"Very good. How about where you are?"

"Ireland."

She looked at the doctor.

"You're in Edinburgh," the doctor corrected. "Do you know why you're here?"

"I'm with Grace."

"When is your birthday?"

"October 7, 1974."

"Good, excellent. We need to keep you overnight, young man." He glanced at Grace. "Just as a precaution."

"But you said it wasn't serious." She'd kick herself if he was seriously injured because she'd flaked out and gone chasing after a ghost.

"I don't think it is. But my recommendation is to let him spend the night to be sure. You may stay for another few hours if you wish." The doctor smiled and left.

She studied Bobby, who didn't seem to have any visible head injury, yet looked out of it. "What happened?" She took a step toward him and he glanced away, out the window. He was angry with her.

"Look, I'm sorry," she said. "I saw this guy who looked like Steven and I thought he'd come over to check on me, but that's impossible because he could never get here that quickly."

"Like the police."

"Excuse me?"

"They showed up too bloody fast." His eyes met hers. "It's like they were around the corner waiting to arrest me. I'm not even sure they were legitimate police."

"Then what were they?"

He closed his eyes.

A few minutes passed in silence.

"Just relax, let them take care of you tonight," she said.

"I can't relax." He pinned her with his dark-brown eyes. "I need to keep you safe."

For a second he sounded as if he cared about her. No, he didn't respect her, didn't think her able to take care of herself. Yet he was the one lying in the hospital bed.

"How did you hurt your head?" she said.

"I don't remember, exactly."

"They claim you fell."

"Against the gravel, yes, I remember that."

"There wasn't any gravel on the sidewalk."

He sat a little straighter and fisted his left hand. His usual expression, one of mild humor, faded and he stared into space as if remembering something.

"Bobby?"

"You need to get me out of here." He pulled the IV needle from his hand and climbed out of bed.

"You sure that's a good idea?" she said.

"I'm fine. I can't be here, especially if they're going to send you home in a couple of hours."

"I can take care of myself."

He shot her a look of disbelief. She was tempted to hightail it out of there, but he'd find her eventually, or worse, chase after her in his hospital gown and get arrested for indecent exposure.

Why did she care? She didn't want his company on this trip.

She stepped outside his hospital room and waited for him to dress. Maybe she didn't welcome Bobby's company, but she'd promised Dad. And in return he'd promised that he'd back off after this trip.

Most twenty-six-year-olds wouldn't care about what their fathers thought, they would have moved far away by now—to the West Coast, or another country even. But Grace has always wanted to please her father, desperate to make him happy because for the longest time he'd always seemed so sad.

Because Mom had died.

Grace couldn't bear to make him angry, to see that

disappointment on his face. He'd frowned at her quite a bit during high school. Even though she'd kept her grades up, she'd had some fun, experimenting with alcohol and boys. She'd had her heart broken in high school when, behind Dad's back, she'd managed to date bad boy Andy Peters. But instead of rubbing it in her face, when Dad found out he only said he was sorry and that although this was her first heartbreak, it would probably not be the last. He held her and told her it would be okay.

Thinking back, he'd always been there for her, when she'd succeeded and when she'd failed, and he'd never made her feel bad about her mistakes.

He'd been a great dad and still was.

Bobby stepped into the doorway and grabbed the frame to steady himself. "Let's go."

He took a few steps and wavered, so she placed his arm around her shoulder and steadied him.

"I can manage," he said, looking down at her.

"I'm sure." She pushed the elevator button and eyed the hallway. No one seemed to notice their escape.

"Did you find him?" Bobby said.

"Who?"

"Your boyfriend."

"No." The elevator door opened.

"Why do you think you keep seeing him?"

"Because I'm a nut. Who knows?" They rode the elevator to the first floor.

Not only was she nuts but she was a liar. She was lying to herself. She kept saying she wanted her independence, wanted to be her own woman and live her own life. Yet even now, in another country, she imagined Steven close by. Why? Because it made her feel more secure.

She'd never be a strong, independent woman this way. Damn, how had she ended up here?

She hailed a cab and they took off for the inn. The charges against Bobby had been dropped once she'd paid for the outfit and explained to the retailer what had happened. She studied him as he stared out the cab window, a dazed expression on his face.

They pulled up to the inn and she helped Bobby upstairs to her room. He kept shaking his head as if he were trying to clear it. She couldn't very well make him sleep on the floor tonight. Maybe she'd get lucky and Mrs. McCarthy would have an opening.

They got to her room and he sat on the floor, tipping his head back against the flowered wallpaper.

She pulled down the covers and turned to him. "Come on, get in bed."

"I'm fine," he said, his eyes closed.

"Right. You could barely make it up the stairs."

He got to his feet and stood firm for a second, then stumbled to the bed. "Bloody hell."

She pulled the covers up to his shoulders, realizing they hadn't found him a change of clothes, save the wild pants and shirt he'd worn out of the store. She doubted he'd put those on again.

Sprawled across the double mattress, Bobby looked like a giant in a junior bed. He rolled onto his side, away from her, and she decided this was the perfect time to make her escape.

She opened the door.

"Don't go," he said.

She hesitated, her hand on the doorknob. "What?"

"Don't…leave."

"I'm just going to get us something to eat. Okay? I'm hungry, it's nearly supper time."

"Grace," he muttered.

Then nothing. She waited a minute.

"Bobby?"

No response. Good, she could zip out and buy him some clothes, then pick up dinner. She left the room, making sure the door was locked.

She walked a few blocks and found a cab to take her to the shopping district. In record time she picked up three pair of jeans and a few plain black shirts. She also picked up underwear and socks, and thought how odd it felt to shop for Bobby. She'd never shopped for Steven.

She picked up a green shirt on sale. Wouldn't hurt to try something different, she thought.

On the way back to the inn she stopped at a pub hoping for some fast, hot food to take back.

Surely food would make Bobby feel better.

Why are you worried about him, girl? He's an employee, not a friend. Heck, she didn't even know him that well.

But she certainly felt ashamed about the incident at the store today. She felt responsible. That's what this was about—making things right. Things were still not quite right with Grace, and they wouldn't be until she finished her quest and found peace.

Sitting on a pub stool, she thought about her plans for tomorrow: Edinburgh Castle. Mom had written about it in her diary, about its great strength and history, about its integrity.

About how she wanted to take Grace there someday.

"I'm here, Mom," she whispered. "I wish you were."

The waitress brought over two boxes of fish and chips, and Grace headed back to the inn. Since it was a beautiful night and not dark yet, she decided to walk to clear her head.

As she walked down Newington Street, she wondered if she could really accomplish what she'd set out to do with Bobby as her shadow. Sure she could. If he'd loosen up a bit, not panic and chase after her wearing a store's merchandise. What was he so worried about, anyway? What could happen to her on a public street in broad daylight?

"Miss?" a male voice said behind her.

She reached for her can of pepper spray, tucked

safely in her pocket. Heck, she didn't even know if the thing shot more than once. In any case, she was ready.

Cripes. Now Bobby was making her paranoid.

She turned and froze at the sight of Harry Franklin smiling back at her.

Chapter Seven

"Didn't expect to see me again, did you now?" Franklin grabbed her wrist.

Grace pointed, sprayed and ran. She heard him coughing, swearing between gut-wrenching gags.

Clutching her bags of clothes and food, she fled from him, determined not to let him take anything from her ever again.

She raced down the street, turned a corner and hailed a cab. She'd get to the inn where she'd call the police immediately. The man who'd assaulted her on the train would not hurt her as he had before.

Adrenaline addled her nerves, and she struggled to remember her destination. "Guest House of Edinburgh," she said.

It was a good mile to the inn, far enough that she felt sure Harry Franklin couldn't follow her. What did he want? He already had her credit cards and money.

The cab dropped her at the inn and she raced up

the stairs. She put down her packages and fumbled in her pocket for her key. Not there. Oh, God, had Harry Franklin picked her pocket when she wasn't paying attention, when she was too busy buying clothes for her bodyguard, buying him fish and chips?

"My key, my key," she whispered, her fingers shaking at the memory of his eyes, dark, like death, with a twisted, sick twinkle in the black pupil.

If he got her key, what else did he get? Could he know where she was staying? They had to get out of here. She knocked on the door and it swung open.

Bobby towered over her, anger filling his eyes. "Where the hell did you go?"

"For clothes, then food, then Harry Franklin found me," she said, her voice catching.

His expression softened and he pulled her into the room with a gentle grip of her elbow. "Slow down, Grace. You saw Harry Franklin? The guy on the train?"

"He was…he was outside the pub—"

"A pub?"

"I went for food, after I got clothes," she said, shoving the shopping bag at him. "I got jeans and shirts and…and…" Her voice hitched.

"Grace, it's okay now. You're safe." Bobby led her to the bed and she sat.

"My key, I can't find my key. What if he got it?"

He unpried her fingers from the food bag and

placed it on the nightstand, then knelt beside the bed and held her hands in his. "Where did you put the key when you left me earlier?"

"Um…jacket, jacket pocket."

"Check it."

She couldn't move, still dazed by the thought that on her one trip out of the country she'd snagged herself a stalker.

But why? She was a middle-school science teacher, for heaven's sake.

"I'm going to search for your key." Bobby reached up and stuck his hand in her left coat pocket. Grace watched his eyes as they filled with concern. If Harry Franklin had taken her room key…

"Not in this one," Bobby said. "Grace, it will be okay. He can't hurt you with me here."

"You were unconscious when I left."

"I'm okay now. Let's check your other pocket."

Something snapped. This is exactly what she'd been fighting: depending on a man to make everything okay.

"No," she said, pushing his hand away. "I'll do it." She reached into her pocket and fished around. If she wanted to be an independent woman she had to start acting like one.

If Harry Franklin had stolen her key she'd just have to deal with it.

Her fingers grazed cool metal. She sighed and pulled the key from her coat pocket.

"It's here. It's fine."

"See? I told you it would be," Bobby said, with compassion in his eyes.

And for some reason she resented it.

She stood and took off her jacket. "I'd better call the police and tell them I saw Harry."

Someone knocked on her door. She jumped back, then took a deep breath and called, "Who is it?"

"Detective Inspector Owen. May I have a word?"

Bobby stood behind the door and motioned for her to open it. She did, and recognized the inspector from the hospital.

"I thought we agreed there'd be no charges brought against Mr. Finn," she said.

"It's not about that. Could you please step into the hall, alone?"

She nodded at Bobby and went into the hall.

"I was about to call the police," she said.

"You were?"

"I just saw the man who attacked me on the train last night. He was following me."

Inspector Owen motioned for her to join him down the hall. "I didn't know you were assaulted. Yes, well, it's beginning to make sense."

"Excuse me?"

"I'm sorry to say that we suspect Mr. Finn may not be the most honorable of chaps."

"Meaning?"

"He has a criminal record, did you know that?"

"I heard something about it." He'd been honest with her and told her about his delinquent teenage years.

"Did you also hear that one of his known partners was a man named Harry Franklin?" Inspector Owen said.

"No." A chill raced down her arms. It couldn't be. Bobby had been hired to protect her. He couldn't have known the man who attacked her.

"Mr. Finn and his partner were suspects in half a dozen burglaries and assaults some years back. Harry got caught and served prison time for one of the crimes, but Bobby Finn's girlfriend provided him with an alibi."

His girlfriend. Of course, always charming the ladies. Charming them into giving alibis, keeping him out of jail. Charming them into buying him clothes, dinner and a place to sleep for the night.

"I…I can't believe it," she whispered.

She glanced down the hall. He was living in her room, touching her things.

She had to get out of here and away from him. Tonight.

Yet something didn't feel right. Dad wouldn't hire a criminal to protect her. Had he been charmed, as well, tricked into hiring Bobby?

"We don't have solid proof of any wrongdoing, but I thought you should be warned," the inspector said.

"Thanks." She wrapped her arms around her stomach.

"He hasn't left your side, has he?" Inspector Owen prodded.

"No. He was supposedly hired by my father as a bodyguard."

"Why would you need a bodyguard?"

"My father is overly protective since I'm his only child." She glanced down the hall. "Why me?"

"Anyone's guess. Is your father wealthy?"

"No, he works as a scientist for the U.S. government."

"Maybe it's about his work. More likely, knowing Mr. Finn's criminal history, it's about money. It's a new angle these days: chum up to a girl on holiday and keep her happy while you blackmail the family."

"But he told me he was with Scotland Yard before becoming a private detective."

"I checked. Couldn't find any record of a Bobby Finn working at Scotland Yard."

Bobby a bad guy, working with Harry Franklin? She should call Dad to see if he'd received a ransom demand.

Damn, her cell phone was in the room.

She'd have to go back in there. Figure out how to get away from him. She should be afraid of him, afraid he might hurt her, but she wasn't. There was something about Bobby Finn, something…gentle.

Get real, girl! Maybe Dad was right to worry about her. She was too darned trusting.

"I appreciate you stopping by."

"I tried phoning but it went into voice mail. You should check your mobile."

"Okay, thanks."

"I'll put out a bulletin on Harry Franklin, see what we can turn up. In the meantime, be wary of Mr. Finn. Oh, he forgot this at the hospital." He pulled a metal cross on a piece of black cord from his pocket.

She took it from him and thought how ironic it was that a man like Bobby Finn would wear a cross around his neck. Yeah, he needed forgiveness for his sins all right.

"Thanks," she said.

"If you need anything—"

"I won't."

He nodded and left. She went back to her room and took a deep, steadying breath before opening the door. Then she had a thought. She started downstairs. Her door cracked open.

"Grace?" Bobby said.

"I'll be right back," she said softly. "I need to find Mrs. McCarthy."

"You won't leave the inn?" He sounded genuinely concerned.

"No," she said, turning and making her way to the first floor. She had half a mind to keep on walking, but her things were in her room, most importantly, Mom's diary.

She needed to get away from all these games and find her mother's hometown. Discover that piece of herself that would make her feel whole.

She found Mrs. McCarthy in the den watching television. "Can I help you?" the woman asked.

"I was wondering if you had any openings tonight?"

"I did have a room open up downstairs."

"I'd like to rent it for my friend," Grace said.

The woman went to the reception desk in the entryway and pulled out a key. She handed it to Grace. "I'll charge your card then?"

"Yes, thank you." Grace went upstairs and opened the door to her room. Bobby was standing by the window, her mother's diary in his hand. She clenched her jaw, suddenly feeling naked.

"That's personal," she said, snatching it from his hands. No one had read Mom's thoughts but Grace. She felt violated and suspicious about his motives.

"I'm sorry," he said.

Like hell, he was. He probably wanted to gain insight into her psyche so he could manipulate her more.

"What did the inspector want?" he asked.

"He needed me to sign a statement about your arrest." *Quick thinking, girl.* She handed him the key. "A room has opened up downstairs."

He took the key and looked surprised, maybe even hurt. "I don't want to leave you."

"I'll be fine. Your room is right by the stairs so you can stay up all night and keep watch if you're that worried."

"You were worried, too, a few minutes ago."

She untied the bag of food, resigned to the fact she'd have to eat this one last meal with him. She didn't want to make him suspicious.

Act cool, unaffected, as if nothing has changed.

"I'm starving," she said. With her foam container in hand she sat on the bed. She took a bite of fish hoping to speed up this process. Inside, her stomach rebelled as she fought her frustration. Was this man her enemy or friend?

No, even if he wasn't her enemy, he wasn't a friend. He was hired to protect her. Maybe. She wasn't sure of anything anymore.

Yet an hour ago *she* was protecting *him* in his hospital bed. Could she really have been so wrong about Bobby? She didn't want to come right out and confront him with the inspector's accusations. She had to figure out another way. She'd start by calling Dad, later, after Bobby left.

She checked her cell phone. The battery was dead.

"You're sure everything is okay?" He walked over to close the door.

"Leave it open," she said. He took a step back and studied her. "Here." She handed him his food. "So, tell me about your work."

"As a private detective?"

She wondered if he was trying to remember which lie he'd told regarding his career.

"That's what you do, right?" she said.

"Yes." He opened his container and analyzed its contents, then closed it. "Maybe later. What else did the inspector say to you?"

He pinned her with those dark eyes of his as if he could read her next lie before she even spoke it. To think she'd thought his eyes warm and charming last night on the train.

"He said they'd put out a bulletin for Harry Franklin. That eased my mind a bit."

"Which doesn't mean they'll find him," he muttered.

Was that wishful thinking?

"Oh, I don't know. Stranger things have happened."

Like I was seduced by a major charmer named Bobby Finn.

"I almost forgot." She pulled the cross from her pocket. "He also came to return this. You left it at the hospital."

He didn't reach for it at first, his expression suddenly younger, a bit lost.

"Thanks," he said, his voice hoarse. He took it from her and placed it around his neck.

"Who gave that to you?" she said.

"My mother, after…" His voice trailed off. "Before I left."

"Left for Scotland Yard?"

"No, left for England, to live with my uncle." He gently rubbed the metal cross as if to conjure good luck or maybe even solace.

That expression on his face made her want to ask more questions about his childhood, his family and his disappointments. Was he really that good an actor?

"Why did you live with your uncle?" she pushed.

Bobby went to the window and stared down onto the street. Why did he live with his uncle? There were so many reasons, all of them rubbish. He knew the truth from the day mum had dropped him with Uncle Thomas: Bobby had been a grand failure and she couldn't stand the sight of him.

She might have tried to whitewash it by saying the schools were better in Uncle Thomas's area of London, and that Bobby needed special help because of a learning problem, but he knew the truth. Ever since Wendy's accident things were not the same at home. Bobby was no longer welcome. It was his fault Wendy struggled to walk with a cane, his fault she'd become a withdrawn, sad woman.

If only he'd been paying attention. If only he'd moved a little faster, Wendy wouldn't have been hit by the speeding car.

And maybe if he'd spent another twenty years solving crimes he'd be able to live with himself.

Or not. He'd never forgive himself for his sister's

condition, always wondering what kind of woman
she would have become if not for the accident.

"Is it for good luck?" she said.

"What?" He'd forgotten what they were talking
about. His brain had been a little fuzzy since his arrest,
and he suspected it was due to more than a slight
knock to his head. Something else had happened when
he was with those two officers. If only he could
remember.

"The cross." She motioned to his neck.

"Not luck, exactly. More like…" What? What
could he say? That it was his constant reminder that
even if his mother and sister couldn't forgive him,
even if Bobby couldn't forgive himself, there was
always hope that God had the compassion to forgive
a bastard like Bobby. "A reminder," he said. "To
behave."

"Does it work?" She smirked.

"Not always."

"Like with women, right?"

"Excuse me?"

"I sense you're a charmer with women. You use
them, right?"

"What if they're using me?" he said.

She shrugged and ate another piece of fish. She
was awfully calm and sure of herself compared to
when she'd come in earlier.

It must have been Owen's visit that had eased her
fear. Even though she had Bobby as her personal

bodyguard, a visit from the local police had probably calmed her down.

Sure it had. Bobby was a failure at protection. She probably sensed it.

"Are you well enough to make it downstairs by yourself?" she said.

"You want to be rid of me that badly?" he joked.

An odd look creased her features as if he'd guessed her very thoughts.

"It's been a full day," she said. "I'd like the rest of the night to myself."

Something was off. She seemed colder, more distant than when they'd gone shopping. He could have sworn they'd developed a connection of sorts this afternoon.

But now, watching the woman on the bed eat her fish and chips, he wondered if he'd imagined it. She suddenly seemed like a complete stranger.

What are you thinking, Bobby? She is *a complete stranger.*

"Have I done something?" he said without thinking.

"Done something?"

"Offended you in some way?"

"No, why?"

"You seem different, uncomfortable."

"I'm tired." She closed her foam container and sighed. "Exhausted from all the drama."

"Right, well…" He started for the door and her

shoulders sagged as if she was relieved. Why? Was she afraid of him?

He thought they'd come to an agreement, an understanding about his role in her holiday. Yet she seemed anxious to be rid of him.

"Good night, then." He opened the door. "Make sure you lock this behind me. And pull the nightstand to the door to block anyone from coming inside."

"The nightstand isn't very heavy."

"The bed then. Something."

"I'll be fine. Will you?"

She said the words, but he sensed she didn't mean them. She wanted him out of her room and quite possibly out of her life.

"Good night," he said.

"Wait." She got up and handed him a shopping bag. "Some clothes I picked up for you."

"Thank you." He closed the door, waited until he heard her lock it and went downstairs to his room. Something felt off, her attitude, her forced smile.

You're suffering from a blow to the head, mate. Maybe it's all in your imagination.

Bobby opened the door to Room Two and flipped on the light. The room was pleasant enough, a wood dresser in the corner and the bed covered with a flowered spread.

He dumped the clothes on the bed. Not bad, he thought. Black trousers, a few black shirts and an emerald-green shirt. Cheeky.

He splashed water on his face at the sink, then dressed in the new clothes.

Well, he couldn't put off the inevitable. Time to call in. He wasn't sure how he was going to break the news to Max that he'd been arrested, although not charged. He'd start by calling Eddie to see if the bloke had any news for him on this case.

"Malone, here."

"Eddie, mate, it's Bobby."

"You okay, man? We got a call from the police asking about your employment with the Blackwell Group."

"Bugger," he swore. "So, Max knows then?"

"Yep. But he thinks something smells fishy, although he didn't say it like that."

"Did you find uncover anything interesting about the Fairmont family?"

"As far as family is concerned, her dad's a scientist, there's an aunt, lives in Madison, and that's about it. Background on the mother, well, Max wants to talk to you about that. But get this: I can't find a record of marriage for her parents. They may not have been married when her mom gave birth to her."

Bobby glanced at the ceiling, picturing Grace sitting in bed, reading her mother's diary. He would bet she didn't know that.

"What else?"

"Couldn't find much on the boyfriend. He must

be a boring kind of guy. He's a financial analyst with Baker and Hughes in Chicago. He brings down six figures easy, doesn't really have hobbies. Just works and hangs out with Grace Fairmont. Oh, and something weird about the mother? The death notice appeared five years *after* she supposedly died in a car accident in the States. I tried finding out more but a virus kept attacking my computer. A symbol would pop up, a pinwheel, you know, the kind that kids blow on to make them spin around? Anyway, the virus would try to eat my hard drive." He paused. "But it couldn't get past Tabitha's chastity belt. Max thought he recognized the symbol. Wait, he wants to talk to you."

Bobby was going to get an earful now. A real thrashing for cocking-up in less than twenty-four hours.

"Bobby, how's it going, mate?" Max inquired.

"It's been better."

"Tell me what's happened so far. In detail."

Bloody hell, he had to relive the embarrassment of this morning?

"Before or after I got arrested for stealing purple trousers?"

"You've *got* to be kidding."

"Wish I were. I'm telling you, guv, this is the strangest twenty-four hours of my life. First Miss Fairmont is attacked on the train, then I sensed the man who picked us up at Waverly was a fake, not with British Transport Police. I got shot with pepper spray last night, then I get knocked unconscious this afternoon while being arrested for stealing purple trousers I didn't even want. Don't ask me to explain that one. Some people don't have this much excitement in an entire year."

He didn't dare tell him he'd lost a chunk of time this afternoon, that he couldn't remember the few hours after the cops arrested him outside the shops.

"Bobby, I'm afraid this case is more complex than we'd originally thought. It's probably best if you bring the girl back to the States."

"She'll never go for it, guv. She's got something to prove to herself, something about her mother."

He thought about the few paragraphs he'd read in the mother's diary, about the love that dripped off the pages. He could understand why she was so determined to walk in her mum's footsteps and absorb some of her personal history.

To be loved like that. With such completeness.

But then, why did the mother leave? That's what it sounded like from Eddie's information.

"It looks like Miss Fairmont's mother was on a British Intelligence watch list of suspected PIRA terrorists," Max said.

"Bloody hell." The Provisional Irish Republican Army.

"I doubt Grace Fairmont is aware of this," Max continued. "What also concerns me is the symbol that kept popping up on Eddie's computer when he tried digging into the mother's background. I recognized it as a code symbol used by British Intelligence. They were key players in the fight against terrorism."

Bobby absently sat on the bed and pressed his fingers to his eyelids. "So, the bloke who picked us up at the train station…"

"Could be MI5 or PIRA. We can't figure out why they'd be interested in the girl. The mother died years ago. Maybe MI5 thinks Grace knows something. It explains why the father has been so overly protective all these years."

"Do you think he knows?"

"I'm not sure. Left him a message, hoping to get answers. Don't mention this to the girl until we know more. The MI5 connection troubles me, but not as much as ties to the PIRA."

Bobby thought about the stolen backpack: stolen, then returned hours later. Was it a ruse by MI5 to plant a bug and track Grace's whereabouts?

"Do you think Grace is in danger, guv?" Bobby squeezed the phone. His protective instincts flared.

"Hard to say," Max admitted. "The mugging on the train could be a part of this, or just bad luck. If he'd been a hired assassin he would have killed her on the spot."

True. Harry Franklin, or whatever his name was, could have ended her life with one slice of a well-placed knife.

A knife…across Grace's throat. That beautiful girl…dead.

"I need to check on her, guv." Bobby hung up and raced to Grace's room.

What was he going to say? Tell her the truth? That her mum had been a PIRA terrorist, possibly under surveillance by British Intelligence? She idolized her mum and trusted her father. She wouldn't believe a word coming out of Bobby's mouth.

He knocked on the door. "Grace? I need to talk to you."

Nothing. He glanced at the bottom of the door. Her room was dark. It was too bloody early for her to have gone to sleep. He knocked again. He had to tell her what they were dealing with, yet he wasn't sure himself.

He persisted, knocking a little louder this time. He didn't want to alarm the innkeeper but couldn't risk Grace's safety.

She still didn't answer. Could someone have broken into her room? Kidnapped her? Killed her?

No, if *they* thought she had information, *they'd* want to keep her alive.

What about the inspector from earlier? Was he legitimate or a fake, planted by MI5? What did British Intelligence want with her? She didn't even know her mother.

Taking the stairs two at a time he started to think

up reasons why he was going to ask Mrs. McCarthy to open the door. He found her in the small den watching news reports on the telly.

"Hello, Mrs. McCarthy," he said, as charmingly as possible, fighting back his panic. "I was wondering if you could check on my friend, Grace."

"Oh, she's fine." The older woman waved her hand. "Left a few minutes ago out the front."

Bobby rushed out the front door to the sidewalk and looked both ways. He spotted Grace walking rather quickly toward the heart of town. Where was she off to? Was she lured out of her room by a mysterious phone caller?

It seemed more likely she was running. From him.

A man approached her and she ducked into a pub. The man kept walking. Bobby followed her and tried to spot her blond hair over the top of the crowd in the pub. She went toward the back door and Bobby caught up to her, placing his hand to her shoulder.

She spun around, her eyes wide with...fear? No, more like anger.

"Blast, Grace, where are you off to alone? It's dangerous. Don't you understand how vulnerable you are, how easily someone could hurt you?"

"Yeah, like you?"

Chapter Eight

Bobby let go of Grace's shoulder. "What did you say?" Good God, she thought *he* was out to hurt her?

"Are you and Harry Franklin working together to blackmail my father?"

"Have you gone completely round the bend?"

"Inspector Owen said there's no record of you working at Scotland Yard."

"Owen? That twit doesn't know what he's talking about. He's probably not even a real detective." He reined in his temper.

"What's that supposed to mean?"

"We need to talk." Bobby glanced at the roomful of pub patrons. Any one of them could be associated with PIRA or MI5.

She took a step away from him. "Just leave me alone, okay?"

"Only if you get back on a plane to the States."

"What? Why? What's your angle now?" She narrowed her eyes at him.

"My angle is to keep you safe. I'm not a criminal. I'm not working with Harry Franklin. Inspector Owen's job is to get me out of the picture, probably so they can get to you."

"*They* who?"

"Please." He motioned with his hand toward a booth. "Sit with me and I'll explain."

She glanced around the room, probably feeling safe because she was surrounded by people, and slipped into the booth. Bobby ordered two pints from a waitress.

"First, I would never hurt you, Grace," he started.

She cocked her chin up as if to say she wasn't stupid. She knew he was lying.

"I don't know Harry Franklin," he said. "Yes, I was arrested when I was a teenager—with a boy named Harry Smith. We were young and stupid and thought we could make a quick hundred quid by breaking into people's homes and stealing valuables. I told you I was a bad kid, Grace. I never lied about that. We all have things in our past we're not proud of."

She sat back in the booth, arms crossed in a defensive posture. He wasn't getting through to her, not even scratching the surface.

But he had to.

"I just spoke with my boss, Max Templeton," Bobby said. "He thinks you could be in danger."

She narrowed her eyes. "Why?"

"Your mother may have been involved with the PIRA when she was younger."

"PIRA?"

"The Provisional Irish Republican Army."

"I don't believe it."

"She was young. People do stupid things when they're young."

Like let their sisters get run down by a drunk motorist.

Grace's gaze drifted to her ale.

"When our computer expert tried to get personal information about your mum he got stumped by a virus," Bobby said. "A virus possibly linked to MI5."

"What's that?"

"British Intelligence. My boss thinks that British Intelligence officers might be keeping you under surveillance."

"Sure they are." She shook her head.

"I'm not kidding," Bobby said, frustrated. What now? Tell her to call her father for confirmation? Bobby wasn't sure Max had spoken to the client about this new development, and Bobby doubted she'd believe anything other than her father's word.

"I'm a science teacher, not a spy or a political figure," she argued. "There's no way British Intelligence would be interested in my boring life."

He sensed pain in her words, regret even.

"You have to consider the fact that your mother's activities have put you in danger."

"No. I don't believe it. My mother was a loving, caring woman. She was not a terrorist."

"Think about everything that's happened since you've been in the U.K. The mugging, the lights going out—"

"Stop," she said. "I'll tell you what. I'm going to leave here and you're going to stay away from me for two reasons: one, if I see you again I'll call Inspector Owen and press charges for harassment, assault and whatever else I can think of to keep you locked up long enough so I can finish my trip. Second, because I'll use the spray again if you don't. I didn't tell you that was my dad's concoction, did I? A mild form of a nerve gas he designed for the military. So unless you want to be using a seeing eye dog for the rest of your life…"

"Grace—"

"Enough. Stay away from me." She stood and marched to the door.

He'd done better when he'd lied to her and charmed her. She wasn't a stupid woman, just misled and frightened.

Right now, of him.

And possibly of the information he'd just shared with her. Somewhere deep down, she had to consider the truth of his words. The reality of a loved one being a terrorist would shatter anyone's world. It would especially shatter the world of a woman seeking answers about her mother…and herself.

He got up and headed for the door. He'd follow her, keep to the shadows and do his job.

Whether she liked it or not.

THE PROVISIONAL Irish Republican Army?

British Intelligence?

Bull.

Bobby was not only charming, but he could lie with such sincerity that she'd nearly believed him.

Shaking off the chill, she headed back to the inn. She'd left earlier to find a public phone since her cell battery had died and the inn phone was just outside Bobby's room. She didn't want him listening in as she called Dad, then other inns to find another place to stay.

Yet, before she could find a phone box and make her calls, she'd sensed someone following her, so she she'd ducked into the pub, filled with people for protection.

That someone had been Bobby, with his outrageous tales and forced concern.

She had to get to a phone and call Dad, had to confirm Inspector Owen's suspicions. Then she'd call other inns. She'd made a mental note of inns she'd seen while shopping today. She'd start with them. She only planned to stay another day to wait for her credit cards.

She found a phone box a block away from her inn and called Dad but got a busy signal. He didn't believe in call waiting. "Focus on one thing at a time," he'd lecture her. She noticed a small black car park across the street and turn off its lights. No one got out.

"Great, now Finn's got you spooked," she whispered to herself.

Pressing the receiver to her ear, she thought about Bobby's wild accusations. Surely Dad would have known if Mom had been involved with a terrorist group, and he would have told Grace.

Then again maybe not. Grace had nothing to hold on to but the faded memory of a loving mother. That's why she felt so empty inside, as if a piece of her was missing. It was all starting to fade, to be lost completely.

Grace was going through an identity crisis, plain and simple.

The things that had once interested her—the opera and playing tennis with Steven—had become boring and routine. To some degree her relationship with Steven had become boring, as well.

Which made no sense at all. He was perfect: solid, steady and he knew what would please her. Steven was the quintessential "perfect" mate.

And she'd been the perfect daughter for Dad.

Suddenly, in her mid-twenties, perfect didn't seem as important as finding answers; finding herself.

She needed her mom.

Since that was impossible, the least she could do was walk in Mom's footsteps, visit the places she'd been and somehow make an emotional connection to give Grace strength to do what she had to: strike out on her own.

Kiss Daddy and Steven goodbye and start a new life somewhere away from them, at least for a while, until she felt like her own person.

"My God, I've really gone…" She hesitated, about to say *crazy* but chose instead "round the bend."

She tried a few inns with no luck. She hung up the phone and decided to go back to her room. Bobby had to know she was serious about reporting him to the police if he attempted to speak with her again.

The flare of a lighter in the car across the street caught her eye.

It had nothing to do with her. The mugging was random, the lights going out were the result of outdated electrical wiring.

What about Mom's picture being stolen? Why steal the photo and not the locket?

She was starting to fall under Bobby's spell, starting to believe his outlandish story about Mom being a terrorist.

You can't run like your mother.

The memory of the mugger's words made her shudder. She'd thought it had been a case of mistaken identity, but if there was any truth to what Bobby had told her...

No, he's liar, a manipulator.

And she had to take care of herself.

She pulled out Inspector Owen's card and called him.

"Owen," he answered.

"Inspector, it's Grace Fairmont."

"Yes, Miss Fairmont, how can I help?"

"I confronted Mr. Finn about his true intentions, and he argued that I was in danger and that my mother had been a terrorist with the PIRA."

"Really?" he said.

"He's lying, of course. But the thing is, I can't find another room for the night and he's staying at the same inn. He's downstairs, but I don't feel entirely safe."

"I'll have him brought in for questioning."

"You can do that? Without me making a formal complaint?"

"We can. I'll send someone over right away."

"He may not be there. I left him at the Royal Oak Pub. I told him if I saw him again I'd press charges."

"I'll post a man outside your inn. Get a good night's rest."

"Thank you, I really appreciate it."

"Would you like me to send a car?"

"That's not necessary."

"Be careful, Miss Fairmont."

"Thanks, I will."

She hung up feeling a bit safer. She'd get to the guest house and lock herself in her room. Then she had to try and get a decent night's sleep. What a joke. How was she going to do that with all this craziness going on around her?

Buttoning her jacket she jogged down Newington Street with one thing in mind: reading Mom's journal. Those pages held the truth, the truth about a loving mother who cherished her baby girl.

Grace sighed. The country. She longed for it, ached to be walking in her mother's hometown of Pitlochry, attend church, visit the sites like Loch Leven Castle and the battleground of Culloden. Mom described these places in her journal as if she'd hoped to take Grace there someday, yet, she almost made it sound as if she was describing the places for the first time, from a tourist's point of view.

There was no sign of anything unusual or threatening as Grace approached the inn. She went inside and was greeted by Mrs. McCarthy.

"Is everything all right? Your father's called twice," the woman said.

"May I use this phone?" Grace motioned to the phone on the cherrywood table.

"Yes. An extra charge for overseas calls."

"That's fine." Grace picked up the receiver and made her call.

"Hello?"

"Dad, it's Grace."

"Thank God."

"I tried calling you but—"

"I was on the phone with the detective agency. They've uncovered some things, some disturbing things. I need to talk to you, Gracie."

No, she didn't want Dad to tell her Mom was a PIRA terrorist under the watchful eye of British Intelligence. Grace wouldn't believe it, not even from Dad.

"She left us, Gracie," he said. "She didn't die in a car accident."

Grace gripped the receiver and stared at the gold-striped wallpaper. She couldn't make sense of his words. Wasn't sure she'd heard him clearly.

"When you were a year old your mom disappeared," he continued. "She left me a note. She asked that I not look for her and begged me to take care of you, explaining how much she loved us both and that was why she had to leave. Five years later someone sent me her death notice from *The Times of London*. She was the innocent victim in a terrorist bombing that killed five people."

"Terrorist bombing? As in…"

"An attempt to kill the prime minister that failed."

"Dad, do you know if she was involved with the Provisional Irish Republican Army?"

"No, I'm sure she was not. Your mother was about peace and compassion. She would never be involved with an organization that hurt innocent people."

"But what do you know about her, really?"

"I know I loved her."

"And she left you. And me. She left us and you never told me."

"I thought you'd be crushed."

"I had a right to know," she declared.

"I'm sorry, Gracie. I couldn't bring myself to tell you the truth. What good would it have done? It doesn't matter now."

"It does, actually. It matters a lot. It means she didn't want me."

"Don't say that, Grace."

"I've gotta go. I love you." She hung up and went upstairs to her room.

Opening her door, she flipped on the light and grabbed the journal off the nightstand.

Her mother didn't want her.

No, Grace refused to believe that.

She locked her door and frantically leafed through the pages, familiar with them all, having committed most of the entries to memory.

> *Grace smiled at me today.*
> *Gracie got her first tooth.*
> *Gracie is such a smart girl.*
> *I can't wait to take Gracie home and show her to my family. I can't wait to show her the hills, the lochs, the beautiful countryside. I love my baby girl so much.*

"Then why, Mom? Why did you leave?"

She snapped the book shut, unable to read another word without bursting into tears of frustration, tears of loss.

It was as if she'd lost her mother all over again, and she didn't even remember losing her the first time.

What had Dad said? That Mom's letter had asked he not try to find her. That she professed her love for both Dad and her baby girl?

Was it simply that she was a member of the PIRA and loved the fight for Irish independence more than she loved her family?

That wasn't possible. Mom was from Scotland; Dad had said so.

He'd also said her mother had been killed by a drunk driver when Grace was a year old. Now that she thought about it, he'd told her *how* mom had died when Grace was twelve, right before the trying years of teenage rebellion and experimentation with alcohol and drugs. Up to that point he'd just said she'd died in a car accident.

Suddenly she felt incredibly manipulated.

Her father had lied to her all these years. Who *could* she believe?

Her heart. Her mother's words. They would lead her to answers. This journey would still give her peace.

Forget the other credit cards. American Express

was good enough for purchases and cash advances. She'd head up north first thing tomorrow.

She needed to prove what she knew in her heart: her mom was not a terrorist. Her mom had loved her. What on earth would have made her run away?

Anger coiled in Grace's chest as she wondered if someone was responsible for chasing her mother away, depriving Grace of her much-needed love.

Grace wanted answers, not only for her identity's sake, but to honor Mom's memory. Grace would uncover the truth.

She glanced down and noticed an envelope had been slipped under her door. She hadn't seen it when she'd come in. Placing the journal on the nightstand, she grabbed the envelope and opened it.

She pulled out a white sheet of paper with three words on it: Please Go Home.

HE LIT a ciggie and glanced at the Guest House of Edinburgh. It would be easy enough to climb in through the window, strangle her and be done with it.

Although it would be rather difficult with agents surrounding the place. Agents and terrorists all out for the same thing: the list. She might have it, or know where to find it. She'd be no use to anyone dead. To think the list could be in the hands of such a naive, fragile creature.

He glanced up the street, wondering if they knew

where she was. She'd run into Franklin earlier, but the team had chased him underground for the time being. Franklin's group had to know she was surrounded by invisible agents.

Yet she was so very alone.

Maybe he shouldn't have eliminated her bodyguard from the equation. He was being paid to keep her safe. But the bloke would complicate the mission with his police instinct and attitude.

This had to go smoothly. For England's sake.

Chapter Nine

Grace hadn't seen Bobby Finn since their blow-up at the pub. She wondered if he'd written the note telling her to go home. Why? To keep her frightened and needy? The door to his room had been shut this morning, and Mrs. McCarthy said she hadn't seen him leave. Grace guessed Inspector Owen had detained him to give her the opportunity to get out of town without being followed.

She was standing in line at the rental car agency when her cell phone rang.

"Hello?" she said. She didn't recognize the caller ID.

"Miss Fairmont? My name is Max Templeton. Your father hired my agency to keep watch over you while in the U.K."

"Yes, he told me."

"I'm wondering if my agent, Bobby Finn, is with you. We haven't been able to reach him on his mobile."

"No, he's not with me. I've asked him to leave me alone."

"I'm sorry? Did he offend you?"

"No, the local police came to see me last night and warned me about him."

"Miss Fairmont, Bobby Finn is a loyal agent and was an excellent inspector with Scotland Yard. I wish you hadn't given him the slip."

"But Inspector Owen said—"

"Forget Owen. He doesn't know the whole picture. Bobby is a determined agent. I'm sure he'll find you. When he does ask him to phone in straight away."

"Anything I should know about?"

"Not at this time. Miss Fairmont, please be careful, pay attention to your surroundings and stay in well-populated areas."

"Thanks."

She pocketed her phone and scolded herself for believing Inspector Owen's tale. What was *his* motivation, she wondered?

Anxious to get out of the city, she signed the rental-car paperwork and found her economy car. She opened the trunk and dumped her bags inside, then got behind the wheel and pulled out her map of the area. She'd just figured out how to get out of town when the passenger door opened. Inspector Owen slid into the car and shut the door.

"What the—"

"Sorry, miss, I don't mean to frighten you, but we lost track of Mr. Finn and I wanted to warn you."

"You could have called the inn."

"You were gone."

"You have my cell number."

"I wanted to speak to you in person."

Stay strong, don't let him sense your fear. Was he even a real policeman?

"You need to know a few things, about your mother," he started.

"You knew her?"

"I knew of her. She was…" he hesitated, "involved in the deaths of innocent people."

"I don't believe you."

"What do you know about her?"

"I know she loved me."

"You didn't know about her affiliation with the Provisional Irish Republican Army?"

"That's not true."

"My organization wants your help."

"Your organization?"

"We need information that we think your mother may have left behind when she died."

"She left me nothing," she said. "Except for a locket and that was broken in a mugging." She wasn't sure why she didn't tell him about the diary. Maybe because it was sacred and she didn't want strangers leafing through it, reading a mother's private thoughts meant for her daughter. Or maybe because he hadn't told her who he worked for.

"I'm sorry, but I don't believe you." He grabbed her wrist and pulled her closer to him. "You need to come with me."

"Let go, you sonofabitch." She squirmed to get away from him.

Suddenly the passenger door opened. Bobby grabbed Owen, pulled him from the car and slugged him twice. The guy fell to the ground in a heap. Bobby raced to the driver's side of the car and opened the door.

"Move over," he ordered.

Stunned, she just looked at Bobby.

"I said *move*." With both hands on her shoulders, he gently slid her over and got behind the wheel. He hit the automatic lock button as Owen got to his feet and pounded on her window.

She shrieked, Bobby put the car in gear and they took off.

"That sonofabitch hurt me," she said, rubbing her wrist with her hand.

"He could have done a lot worse. What were you thinking, running off on me this morning? You could have been killed."

"I thought you were the bad guy, remember?"

"Oh, I'm bad, Grace, that's true. But I'm not the one trying to hurt you."

"I know." She hugged herself and glanced out

the window. "Max Templeton called my cell looking for you."

"Bugger, that can't be good news. I'm taking you to Heathrow."

"No, you can't."

"This isn't a simple holiday anymore. This is about terrorists and spies and who knows what else."

"They'll find me back in the States, too. We need to get answers, find out what my mom was about. It's the only way I'll be truly safe."

"No, you're going back."

"Dammit, Bobby, I've come this far. I'm too close to give up."

"What's so bloody important that you'd risk your life to go touring the countryside?"

"My life. Finding out who I am and why." She paused. "Why Mom left."

"She died. People die. It happens."

"But she didn't just die. She left us when I was a year old. She died years later. I need to know why she left. I need to know who she was."

"What difference does it make?"

"I guess not a lot to someone like you. You know who you are and what your mission is in life: finding bad guys, protecting good girls." She sighed. "But I'm lost, Bobby. I've been lost for a long time, and the only way I'm going to find myself is by getting some answers."

"You're putting yourself at risk."

"I'll be at risk no matter where I am. I can't stop that now. I've opened some kind of door to danger that only I can close. You've got to help me. Please."

Bobby didn't say anything at first. He still couldn't believe her determination to continue this trip after her encounter with Owen. Was he MI5, or with the PIRA? What did they want with her?

He took a deep breath and headed north out of town. They'd have to ditch the car if they didn't want to be followed. Owen could have put a tracking device on it.

He glanced at Grace, then back out the front window. Bugger, she could have been hurt. But if they'd wanted to hurt her, wouldn't they have done it already? And who were *they*? He wouldn't mind answers himself.

But not about his identity or his mother. He had all those. He knew the sins he'd never shake loose from his soul.

Yet Grace seemed wounded by the news that she'd been abandoned. It was fresh in her eyes, shadowing the blue with a hint of sadness.

And it resonated someplace deep in his chest.

"I need to speak with Max," he said. "The battery is dead on my mobile. May I use yours?"

"Sure, I can call for you."

"Thanks."

"I'm sorry," she said.

He glanced at her.

"I'm sorry I believed that jerk over you," she said.

"Forget it. I wouldn't have believed me, either."

"Why do you do that?"

"What?"

"Beat yourself up like that?"

"Habit. Phone Max, will you?"

She hit redial for the last incoming call and held the phone to his ear. "It's Bobby," he said, when the phone was picked up.

"We've been worried. Everything okay?"

"Fine. I'm with Grace."

"Brilliant, I knew you'd find her," Max said.

"She was nearly taken by a bloke pretending to be a detective in the Edinburgh police."

"What was he looking for?"

"Not sure."

"After we hang up, talk to her and find out what he asked her. We're still unclear about why this has all surfaced at this time in her life."

"Maybe because she's in the U.K?"

"Possibly."

"Isn't it the middle of the night there?"

"Early morning, actually," Max said. "I couldn't sleep. I never sleep well when Cassie's away. She's visiting her mum."

"Miss your security blanket, do you?" Bobby joked.

"That, and I'm worried about this case. Eddie was up all night digging for clues. Not that he sleeps much."

"No, only at his desk."

"Here's what we know: Miss Fairmont's mother, Mary Logan, was affiliated with the PIRA when she was a teenager and then into her twenties. But what's odd is that her parents moved to Scotland when Mary was eighteen, during the prime of her activity. She accompanied them, yet spent half the year back in Ireland with relatives. Then she disappeared from the U.K. when she was twenty-three and ended up in the States where she struck up a romance with Don Fairmont. Two years later, she gave birth to Grace. About a year after that she left them to go back with PIRA in Ireland. She was killed in a parade bombing five years later."

"So, she's gone, it should be over." Bobby glanced at Grace, who studied him with such intense blue eyes.

"But it's not," Max said. "It doesn't tally, mate. There's more to this woman's life and I suspect it's dangerous. Are you putting Miss Fairmont on a plane home?"

"She won't go."

"I was afraid of that."

"She says the trouble will follow her back to the States as long as this is unresolved." He glanced at her and nodded. "She's got a point, guv."

"Yes, now that Pandora's box has been opened we'll have to deal with it. We'll keep digging, see if we can turn up anything to help you arm yourselves."

"Yes, sir."

"Don't let her out of your sight."

"I won't."

"Has she accepted that you're the agent sent to protect her, not some phony?"

"I think so."

"Bobby?"

"Yes?"

"There's no one I'd rather have watching Miss Fairmont."

"Thanks, guv."

"Be careful."

"I will."

Bobby nodded to Grace to hit End, and took a deep breath. What had started as a babysitting assignment had turned into international terrorism and possibly espionage. What was MI5's angle? Did they think her mother might still be alive and they hoped to use Grace to lure her out?

No, by all official accounts Mary Logan had died in the parade bombing. Yet what if she wasn't simply a soldier for PIRA? What if there was more to this intrigue?

"Go on, I can handle it," Grace said.

"I'm sorry?"

"You have this look on your face like you're afraid to tell me something."

"I'm thinking."

"You're stalling. Please, don't keep things from

me. I feel like everyone's been keeping the truth from me my whole life. If there's one thing I won't forgive it's people keeping the truth from me ever again."

"We have some facts but not much confirmation."

"What facts?"

"Are you really up for this?"

"Please."

"Fact: your mum was with the terrorist group PIRA as a teenager and up through her twenties. Fact: she came to the States for a few years in the later 1970s, for what reason, we're not sure. That's when she met your father. She went back to PIRA in 1981 and was killed in a bombing in '86. We think both PIRA and British Intelligence are interested in you, her daughter."

"I feel like I don't even know my own mother," she whispered. "But why is this happening now?"

"Did you make inquiries about your mother before you came to the U.K.?"

"Well, sure, I had to find out where she grew up, if she had family, all that stuff."

"You must have accidentally alerted PIRA to your existence. What I can't figure is what they want from you."

"That makes two of us."

"What did that Owen bloke say to you?" Bobby pushed. "You need to remember every word if possible."

"He asked if my mother had given me anything. I said yes, the locket."

"Did you tell him about the diary?"

"No." She turned to him and held his gaze. "I don't know why. It's silly, I guess, but Mom's diary is private. It's the only thing I have of hers that shows me how much she loved me."

If she'd loved Grace she wouldn't have abandoned her, Bobby thought. The lost look in her eyes made him keep that opinion to himself.

"Was there anything in the diary explaining why her family moved to Scotland?"

"No. She started this diary when she was pregnant with me. She wrote down stories about her childhood and her homeland though."

"Ireland?"

"Scotland. She's from Scotland, that's why the PIRA stuff doesn't make sense."

"She's Irish, Grace. Her family moved to Scotland when she was a teenager."

She leaned back against the seat. "Everything is a lie," she said. "Do you think we'll find any truth in all this?"

"Yes. It may not be the truth you're looking for, but it's there."

"I wanted answers so badly, hoping they would make me whole. Yet all I feel right now," she hesitated, "is ashamed."

"Why?"

"My mother was involved in killing innocent people."

"We are not our parents, Grace." He tried to believe the words as he spoke them, tried to believe he wasn't a failure to his family like his father: a man who abandoned a wife and five children for the sea.

"What would make someone do that?" she said.

He pulled into a parking lot of another car-rental agency to switch cars. "Make someone…"

"Join a terrorist group."

"They don't consider themselves terrorists. They feel passionate about their cause," he said.

Bobby was starting to feel passionate about protecting Grace. This young woman was faced with a complete upheaval in her life, new information that could forever change her future. Yet he sensed she was determined to deal with it and come out a stronger person.

He'd never known a woman quite like her. Bobby chose to sleep with scatty types who were drawn in by his looks and charm. That was the difference. He wasn't going to sleep with Grace.

Bobby wasn't stupid. He knew the worst pain was caused by love. He'd read that pain in his own mother's eyes with each year that his father stayed away. He'd broken her heart and she'd become a sad, semi-functional woman.

Bobby had no plans to tangle with the romantic type of love.

He could imagine plenty of blokes falling head over heels in love with Grace Fairmont. It was her innocent smile and determination, and maybe even that edgy vulnerability that gave the impression she didn't mind a strong man in her life as long as he respected her independence.

"Why are we here?" she said, glancing across the car-rental lot.

"Need a different car. Don't want to be followed into the country."

Although Bobby knew if MI5 was interested in her, there wasn't much to keep them from finding Bobby and Grace.

Outsmarting British Intelligence? How was Bobby going to do that?

He told her to stay in the car and lock the doors while he rented another car. At least they would reduce their chances of being tracked up north. He got the new car then checked her backpack for a tracking device. Nothing.

Then again, if British Intelligence had known what train Grace would be on two nights ago, they'd surely know where Grace was headed—to her mother's hometown.

Everything Bobby did, he did with Grace in mind. *Of course. Because that's your job, mate. Think of her needs first and put her safety ahead of everything.*

He found A90 and headed north.

"Did you always know you wanted to do this?" she said.

"What, chaperone beautiful women around the countryside?" he joked. She looked so sad and lost. He wanted to brighten her cheeks, maybe even make her smile.

"Beautiful, huh?" she said.

"You're fishing for more compliments, are you?" She smiled.

His heart filled his chest. Bugger, she was dangerous in a completely innocent sort of way.

"By the way, nice shirt," she said. He heard the humor in her voice.

"Thought I'd try something different," he said. This morning, he'd put on the green shirt she'd bought him.

"Were you always interested in police work?" she asked.

"Actually, no. I figured I'd be in jail by the time I turned twenty. Instead, Max demanded I make something of myself. He's like a father figure, but don't tell him I said that. He's barely ten years older. I think he'd be offended."

"What happened to your father?"

Bobby could feel his smile fade.

"He's gone, isn't he?" she said.

"A long time ago," Bobby answered.

"How did he die?"

"He didn't. He left. Left my mother with five children under the age of eleven. I was the oldest."

"That must have been a big responsibility."

"It was, until I cocked-up and she sent me away." Why couldn't he shut his mouth?

"Cocked-up? What does that mean?"

He glanced at her then back to the road. "It means my little sister was hit by a car and it was my fault."

Chapter Ten

She studied Bobby's expression, his set jaw and dark penetrating eyes focused on the road. She sensed he hadn't meant to let the information slip about his sister, about his own perceived failure.

"I'm...I'm sorry," Grace said.

Still, how could an eleven-year-old boy be expected to take care of four younger children?

"It was a long time ago," he said.

Yet he wore it like a favorite jacket, slipping into it daily. Kind of like his cross. Did that reminder have something to do with his sister?

"How were you responsible?" she pushed.

"I'm her older brother. I should have stopped Wendy from going out into the street."

"Accidents happen, Bobby."

"Not this one. It could have been prevented."

I failed. He might as well have said the words.

Suddenly she realized why protecting her was so

important. He was trying to right the wrongs of his past by keeping her safe.

"Thanks, by the way," she said.

"For what?"

"For finding me today; for putting up with my suspicions about you being the bad guy."

"It's important to be suspicious." He paused. "Of everyone."

He was warning her to keep her distance. Why? Did he think she was going to fall for him, on vacation?

"I should call Steven," she said, giving the not-so-subtle hint that her heart belonged to another man, even if she wasn't entirely convinced of it herself.

And maybe it would remind her, as well, because in the past few days she'd found herself attracted to Bobby Finn. Of course she had; he was a real charmer. His natural charisma drew women to him, his smiles, his sense of humor.

Was any of it real? Or was it an act to do his job?

God, she was so desperate for "real." Starting with the truth about her mom.

She called Steven, but again, her call went into voice mail.

"Hey, Steven," she said. "I'm okay now, heading up to Pitlochry for the week. We've got a lot to talk about when I get home." She glanced at Bobby, who pretended not to be listening. "I've learned some things about my mom that are a bit unsettling. Anyway, not to worry. I'm safe. Well," she hesitated, unable to the say the three words shared by lovers. "Talk to you soon."

She slipped the phone into her pocket and glanced out her window. It's not like they had said I love you all the time. No, it was more like a casual love-ya type of endearment, like punctuation on the end of a sentence: necessary and expected.

Of course it was expected. They'd been going out for more than a year, took turns sleeping over on weekends and watered each other's plants when one of them was out of town.

If you disregarded the sexual relations, they sounded more like friends than lovers. Not that she'd know what true lovers acted like. Sure, Dad loved Andrea but Grace always sensed his one true love had been Mom. Mom had drawn out his uninhibited passion and filled his heart completely.

Truth was, Steven didn't do that for Grace. He was nice and courteous and said all the right things, almost as if he'd read a book on how to please a woman. Yet it didn't fill her up.

The thought of living with him for the rest of her life didn't excite her.

Not nearly as much as the thought of Bobby Finn touching her.

Oh, crud, not good.

Being attracted to her bodyguard was disastrous for so many reasons starting with the fact that he was with her because of his job, not because he wanted to be with her. Secondly, wasn't there a name for the warped syndrome of a woman being attracted to her bodyguard? It was a natural progression created by a dangerous situation. This relationship wasn't real any more than the charming ways of the man sitting next to her. His charm was a well-practiced act, she guessed, to get his way with women.

What was really buried beneath his casual charm? *Forget it, girl. You're looking for trouble if you go digging for that answer.*

"I've had some karate training," Bobby said.

She snapped her gaze to meet his. "What?"

"You look worried about me protecting you. I don't need a weapon to defend myself."

Yeah, but how was she going to defend herself against the simmering attraction growing between them?

She'd rely on his honor. He was a gentleman. She could tell by the way he had touched her after she'd seen Harry Franklin. Bobby had knelt in front of her and soothed her nerves by cradling her hands in his. When he'd searched in her pocket for the key, he'd been so gentle, his eyes warm with comfort. And at the pub, when he'd caught her running away, he'd put his hand to her shoulder to stop her.

A gentle hand.

A comforting hand.

Even when he'd been upset with her.

"Look, if you're that worried we'll stop before we get to town and I'll show you a few moves," he said.

"Moves?" Like hugging, kissing, touching in the most intimate of places?

"So you can protect yourself in case we're separated," he explained.

SHE WAS TOO QUIET, Bobby thought an hour into the drive. Something was on her mind. He hoped he hadn't said anything to upset her. She had enough to deal with, especially the potential danger of being watched and hunted.

Was it something the phony inspector had said that had upset her?

He watched her turn a page in the diary, reading intently. "I need to ask you something," he said.

"Sure." She glanced up.

Those blue eyes, so wide and innocent, made his heart race a bit, like when he'd had a crush on Molly Longergan in grade school.

You weren't good enough for her and you're surely not good enough for Grace Fairmont.

"Can you remember anything else the Owen bloke said to you?" he asked.

"Other than Mom being involved with the deaths of innocent people?"

"He said that?"

"Yes."

Then he had to be British Intelligence.

"Did he give you any indication what he wanted from you—" Bobby paused.

"When he practically ripped my hand off?"

He noticed the rise in the pitch of her voice but it was not from fear. She was angry. Good, anger would keep her sharp.

"I'm sorry I didn't get to you sooner," Bobby said.

"You should hardly feel sorry. I ditched you, re-member?"

He shot her a pleasant smile, not the one he used when flirting. Grace wasn't a female to warm his bed. She was an intelligent girl on the run, trying to sort out her past.

A girl in danger.

"In case you get the urge to ditch me again, I've got an idea." He pulled off the side of the road into a gravel drive. "It's time for that self-defense lesson."

He parked and got out of the car. She joined him in a grassy area and stood there, impatient.

"What, you don't think this is important?" he said.

She leaned against the hood of the car. "You're always going to be with me, so what's the point?"

Not always, luv.

"It will be good for you to know, regardless. Pay attention. First, always be aware of your surround-ings. If you sense something's off, change direction and be ready to run or find a policeman to help."

She made a face.

"Okay, maybe not a policeman but get into a large crowd. Generally, you're safe when you're surrounded by people."

"And if I'm alone in the middle of nowhere?" She motioned to their surroundings.

"Keep eye contact. Don't show any weakness. Think of everything as a weapon. Your objective is to survive and get safely away. That's the only rule. Scream, bite, scratch, kick, do whatever you have to. Think about things you have on you as weapons."

"I've still got some pepper spray left."

"Excellent. Look around you, everything here can be used as a weapon: dirt, stones, bricks. You have to train your mind to think differently about everything you see. You don't have time to consider if you should or shouldn't. We know we're being followed so take action immediately."

She nodded. Determination flared in her eyes. Good, she was ready.

"How about some physical moves?" he suggested.

"Sure," she said.

He could have sworn she blushed. *Focus, mate. You've got to teach her to protect herself.*

He got behind her and wrapped his arm around her neck. "I'm going to take your money," he whispered into her ear. "Kick me," he ordered.

She did, half-heartedly.

He released her and turned her around to look at her. "Are you playing with me? Come on now, this isn't fun and games."

"I don't want to hurt you."

"You won't." He turned her around and wrapped his arm around her neck again. "I'm going to take your mum's diary."

She kicked, swung her arms up to hit his head, and he lost his balance. They both went down, Grace on top of him, snickering.

And it angered him.

"This is serious business," he said, unable to keep the irritation from his voice. "This is your safety we're talking about."

She stopped abruptly and cleared her throat. "Sorry, I laugh when I'm embarrassed."

She was leaning on him, like a girlfriend leaning across her boyfriend's body at a picnic. Close, so very close. His breath caught in his throat. How could he be this close and not kiss her? Her tongue licked her bottom lip. Blast, he was going to lose it in a minute. He struggled to hold on to his self-control.

This was not a one-nighter like the rest. She was his assignment, a woman he had to keep safe. He'd have a heck of a time concentrating on her safety if he was kissing her.

"If you don't, I will," she said.

He studied her eyes, filled with need. "Will what?"

She leaned forward and kissed him, the taste so bloody perfect. He'd never paid attention to the taste of a woman's lips before. It never seemed to matter. Just kiss her, get her into your bed, feel the connection for a brief few minutes, then detach. Don't think about how soft her lips felt or how delicious their taste.

Grace's lips were bloody amazing.

And he'd gone completely mad.

She opened her lips to tease him, tasting him, flirting with him. He couldn't control his arousal, his need for this woman.

No, it was a natural response. He'd be hard like this with any woman who lay across his chest, kissing and touching. She slipped her fingers into his hair, the touch so utterly sensual, erotic.

She's throwing herself at you because you're her protector and she's scared.

It wasn't like he hadn't been used before to pump up a woman's ego by making her feel desired. It had never mattered before. They'd both gotten what they needed: the woman got her ego stroked and Bobby enjoyed physical warmth for a few hours. But this time…

Holding her by the shoulders, he broke the kiss. "Stop."

Her cheeks reddened as she looked at him with confusion mixed with need. He didn't read either gratitude or fear in her eyes.

No, he read desire.

For him.

"Did I misread you?" she said. "Oh, my God, I did. I'm an idiot."

She got to her feet and ran her hands through her hair. Bobby sat up and watched her go through a range of emotions from panic to embarrassment to hurt.

He didn't mean to hurt her. It was a mistake; a misunderstanding.

She misunderstood the need in your eyes? Not likely.

"I hate lies, Bobby," she said, suddenly, facing off at him. "My whole life seems like one big lie right now. Don't lie to me and tell me I misread the signals."

"You didn't." He stood and brushed off his jeans. "I'm attracted to you. You're a beautiful woman." He hesitated, hoping his next words would make her want to stay away from him—for her own good. "It's a normal reaction, especially with you throwing yourself at me."

"What?" She planted her hands on her hips. "I don't think so. You wanted to kiss me first."

How ridiculous, Bobby thought, the two of them acting like children arguing about who started a fight. Only there was a lot more at stake than who would stay after school for punishment.

Her safety was at stake. Her life.

And Bobby's heart.

What are you thinking about, mate? You can't act on your attraction if you want to keep her safe. It would be too distracting.

Not to mention complicated. When this case was finished, she'd fly back to her American boyfriend and Bobby would be…where? Alone, again, bedding scatty blondes.

As opposed to the blonde who stared him down, wanting him to admit his attraction to her.

"We need to go." He walked toward the car.

"You need to apologize," she said.

"For what?" He reached for the door and she blocked him.

"For being a jerk."

"I'm not going to apologize for who I am."

"And who is that exactly?" she said.

"I'm a ladies' man. I draw women like honey draws flies." He leaned forward, their faces merely touching. Her eyes widened. "I'm not your boyfriend, Grace. I'm the devil when it comes to women. Don't forget that."

He snapped the door open and her shoulders jerked, but she held his gaze. Tough little American girl. Good, she'd need that strength to protect herself.

From her pursuers.

And from Bobby. Because he wasn't sure how long he could be her companion without touching her blond waves, without losing himself inside her. Completely.

She broke their staring match and fully pushed open the door, nearly hitting Bobby. Good, maybe he'd angered her enough that she'd stop looking at him with compassion in her eyes and stop speaking to him in that gentle, sweet voice.

She pulled her door shut before he could do the gentlemanly thing and shut it for her.

This is best, mate. For everyone.

He got behind the wheel and steered the car toward her mother's hometown. She leaned her head back against the seat rest, closed her eyes and turned her face away from him, her blond waves covering her beautiful pale skin.

He gripped the steering wheel and focused on the road, on getting them to Pitlochry.

Bugger, this was all wrong. Insanity. He should have put her on a plane to America.

Why hadn't he?

Because he knew she wouldn't go. Or was it something else? The longing he read in her eyes whenever she spoke of her mother?

Is that really it, Finn? Or is it your personal desire to spend time with her, bask in the warmth of her gentle energy? He thought about her mood before their shopping trip had gone terribly wrong. She'd been over the moon with everything she had purchased. He'd never known anyone generally happy with life, so open with her thoughts and feelings.

Bobby protected his feelings beneath an armor

of smart-aleck comments and forced laughter. His feelings were ugly and sordid, not to be shared with anyone, ever.

Except for the one time he'd been arrested by Max. Bobby had fought by completely shutting down, and Max had poked and prodded until Bobby finally had exploded into a mass of pain, all the disappointments of his life tumbling out of his mouth; tears floating down his cheeks.

That was the second time in his life he'd cried. The first had been after Mum had left him with Uncle Thomas. Bobby had never felt more alone in his life.

It had been his own fault. He was a bad seed, a worthless big brother.

But he wasn't going to be a failure as a detective. Which meant he'd have to keep Grace safe.

He looked over at her. She'd opened her eyes and was leafing through her mum's diary.

"What's next?" he said.

She turned to him and her eyes seemed bloodshot. Bastard, had he made her cry?

He snapped his gaze back to the road.

"Next?" she questioned.

"We get to Pitlochry and then what?" he said.

"We find my family, or rather, Mom's family. I wouldn't mind stopping along the way first. Mom wrote about a place in her journal I'd like to see."

"Sightseeing," he muttered.

"I don't like this," she blurted out.

"Me, either."

"I'm referring to you acting like such a jerk."

"It's—"

"Don't say it. I don't believe it's who you are, Bobby. I think you act like a jerk to keep people away. I'm not going to hurt you. I have no reason to hurt you."

But you kissed me. And it wasn't a simple kiss, a one-nighter kiss. It got to me, shot panic through my nerves. You got through.

"Bobby?"

He didn't respond. What could he say?

They continued their drive in silence, until she pointed out a spot written about in her mother's diary. He pulled over and she got out.

"Are you coming?" she said.

"I'm fine right here." He stared out the front windshield.

She sighed, grabbed the diary and left. He watched her sit down and gaze across Loch Leven at a ruined castle on an island. With hands braced to the ground, she leaned back and soaked up the sunshine.

He wanted this assignment over, so he could get back to his real work: finding criminals.

There's no one I'd rather have watching Miss Fairmont.

Max might change his mind if he knew how Bobby was struggling to keep this a professional relationship.

Relationship? Is that what you called it?

After twenty minutes or so, Grace stood and walked back to the car. Good, they could move on. She got in and shut the door, clearing her throat.

"It's just as she'd described it," she whispered. "She came here with her grandmother once. Mary, Queen of Scots, was imprisoned in the castle. She escaped with help from her jailer's son who had fallen in love with her."

"Shall I drive on?"

"In a second. I want to savor the moment of being where Mom was. To breathe in the same air." She glanced at Bobby. "You wouldn't understand."

No? How many times had he wished for the chance to head out to sea, feel the sea air slapping his face as it did his father's nearly every day of his life?

"We can go," she said, readjusting herself to face forward.

He put the car in gear, a part of him wanting to tell her he *did* know how she felt, that he knew the ache of wanting to make a connection with someone so badly that you could barely breathe.

More silence. He couldn't stand it. He didn't want to be at odds with Grace. He just didn't want her getting too close.

"I think I do understand," he said.

"Yeah, then explain to me why I'm so scared."

"No one will hurt you, Grace. Not while I'm around."

"That's not what scares me," she said. "I'm scared to meet them."

"Your family?"

"What if they don't accept me?"

"Why wouldn't they?"

"I'm American, for one."

"That's not your fault," he joked. He pulled into town and looked for East Moulin Road.

"What if they don't know about me?"

"Highly unlikely."

"Or they don't…" she hesitated, "…like me."

"How could they not? You're a smart, witty, beautiful girl." He pulled up a long drive to a rather large bed-and-breakfast owned by her family.

"Yeah, you're paid to say things like that."

"I'd say them anyway," he let slip.

He found a parking spot outside the house.

"I don't know, Bobby." She eyed the house through the front window, nibbling at the side of her lip.

Bloody hell, he wanted to touch her, chase away whatever fears were making her nervous.

He got out of the car and opened her door. "It will be fine, Grace. I'm sure they'll love you." He smiled and extended his hand.

She took it and he pulled her out of the car. It was strange how she held on to it as he shut her door and stranger that when he let go she still stayed close.

He sensed her fear and he understood it. What

would his father say to him if he saw him again after all these years? Bobby didn't want to think about that. He'd failed his family and didn't need his father's condemnations to pound that into his soul.

"I should have called," she whispered.

"No, but don't be alarmed if they're distant. You don't know if they know about you, how they felt about your mother's—" he hesitated and looked into her eyes "—possible involvement with the PIRA."

"I know that's not true. I know it in my heart."

"Good. Hold fast to that knowledge. In the meantime," he said, glancing back at the house, "it's time to meet your family."

"Stay close," she said.

"If you wish."

"I order. My dad's paying your salary, remember?" She shot him a nervous smile.

She started toward the house and he walked alongside her. She slowed as she reached the front door.

"Steady now," he whispered. "You're a brave girl. I know you can do this."

She reached out to knock and the door swung wide-open. A young couple breezed past, holding hands and nuzzling one another. Bobby encouraged her to forge ahead.

They went into the house, and Grace paused in the entryway. Looking around, taking it all in. Bobby assumed she was sensing her mother's presence here.

"Hello," a woman said, walking up to them.

"Hi, I'm Grace Fairmont. My mother was Mary Logan."

The woman narrowed her eyes at Grace and took a step closer. "If you know what's good for you, you'll turn around and fly back to America."

Chapter Eleven

Grace's heart plummeted. "Excuse me?"

"You heard me," the older woman hissed.

"Hold on there," Bobby said.

"Lydia!" a woman called, walking into the hall-way. "Welcome," she said, turning her attention to Grace and Bobby. "Did you have a reservation?" She stepped in front of the older woman and gestured for her to leave.

The woman harrumphed and disappeared into the kitchen, but not without one last sneer. Great. This was a horrible mistake.

Bobby touched Grace's shoulder as if he'd read her trepidation, then turned to address the second woman, a redhead who looked to be in her mid-thirties.

"Miss Fairmont has come from the United States to track down family. Her mother's last name was Logan?"

A look of surprise lit the woman's face. "Your

mother? Your mother was Mary Logan? Mary Logan was my aunt. That's fantastic!" She gave Grace a hug, then stepped back. "I don't believe it! I never knew my aunt had a daughter. I'm Anne, your cousin. I'm so stunned."

Anne had reddish hair, like Mom had had, but other than that, Grace didn't notice much of a resemblance.

"Out of nowhere you show up?" Anne said. "How wonderful."

"I'm glad you think so." Grace glanced toward the kitchen.

"Oh, don't mind Lydia. She's a little touched in the head, but she makes delicious cakes. Who's this, your boyfriend?"

Grace started to correct her, but thought better of it. How would she explain Bobby's presence without alarming the family?

"This is Bobby Finn."

"Good to meet you," he said.

"Ah, that's an interesting accent," Anne commented.

"Originally from Ireland," he explained. "Moved to London as a boy."

"We met in London, actually," Grace said. "On business." Great, she'd just met her new family member and was already lying.

Bobby smiled at her. "Grace has been talking about visiting her mother's home town for months now."

"And I'm glad you came." She smiled. "I'm having a hard time wrapping my head around it. You'll have to forgive me."

"I should have warned you," Grace said.

"Well, let's get you two settled so you can rest up from your trip."

"May I ask," Grace started, following Anne to a small office off the main hallway, "are there other family members here? My grandparents?"

Anne's dark-green eyes met Grace's. "I'm sorry, they're gone. But your Aunt Rosie and Uncle Gerry live here, that's my mother and father. They run a shop in town and will be back for dinner. She's going to be so excited to see you."

"Thanks." Grace glanced at the artwork on the walls. "My mom lived here?"

"She did, yes. When she wasn't in Ireland."

Grace sensed something in the woman's voice.

Anne pulled a key from the top drawer of her desk. "We can catch up on all that later. I've got a cousin from America," Anne said, awe in her voice. "Let's get you settled. Have you got luggage?"

"I'll get it," Bobby offered.

"Meet us upstairs," Anne directed, then motioned for Grace to join her.

Grace started up the stairs and heard the door to the kitchen creak open. She spotted Lydia peeking through the doorway. The woman did not like her. Not one bit.

But she didn't even know Grace. Maybe it was resentment about Mom. She must have been a handful growing up.

"Your mother lived here until her twenty-second birthday, then she went to America to find the man of her dreams," Anne said.

"My father."

"We received a postcard periodically. Then nothing. Then we were notified of her death in London. It didn't make sense, why she was back in the country and we hadn't heard from her. Grandmother never quite got over that."

I haven't gotten over the fact I lost my mother, seemingly before she was killed.

"You have no idea why she came back?" Grace pushed.

"I'm not much for gossip."

"Gossip?"

"Here's your room." Anne paused at a door and stuck the key in the lock. She shot Grace a sympathetic smile. "There were rumours about your mum's involvement with a radical group. But your mother's gone. We should all move on."

If only Grace could.

Anne opened the door and Grace stepped inside a room decorated in Victorian style, with lace pillow covers and flowered curtains.

And one bed.

Luckily it had a private bath, so she wouldn't be

stuck in a bathroom down the hall with the lights out again. No, she'd be stuck sharing a room with Bobby Finn.

"I'll leave you to rest up," Anne said. "I'd love to stay and chat but I have rooms to ready for today's new guests. I keep this one reserved for special friends." She smiled and gave Grace another hug. "I'll check back when I can. Supper isn't until seven, so why not take a walk down to the village, or drive out to the Pass of Killiecrankie? We'll catch up later. The family will be so excited to meet you."

"Thanks," Grace said, suddenly hating her midwestern accent.

Anne left and minutes later there was a knock.

"Room service," Bobby called through the door.

Graced opened the door and he stepped into the room carrying the luggage. "Nice room," he said.

"I guess you expect a tip?" she joked.

"No, just loan me a pillow from your bed, and maybe a blanket if you can spare one."

She went to the window and hugged herself. Glancing across the rolling countryside, she wondered which room Mom had slept in. Had she walked the green hills that seemed to stretch for miles? Grace loved being outside basking in sunshine. Was she like her mother in that respect?

"You can keep your pillows," Bobby said, walking up to her. "I'm sure they have extras."

She glanced at him. "No, it's fine. You can have whatever you need."

What Grace needed was to have Bobby's arms around her right now to absorb some of his strength. She could use a friend.

Bobby would quickly become more than that, she sensed. He'd already lit something inside her that had made her kiss him a few hours ago. If he got too close she was going to do it again.

"Stop looking at me like that," he said. His soft brown eyes grew dark, more intense.

"Like what?" she said.

"You know like what."

"I'm sorry." She ripped her gaze from his and hugged herself tighter. "I guess it's all these emotions flooding to the surface. Being in Mom's home."

He wrapped his arms around her and squeezed. She leaned into him, as she'd wanted to before, welcoming his strength to hold her up. Because, right now, she was dangerously close to dissolving into a puddle on the floor.

"What is it?" he asked.

"Everything."

"Your cousin seems nice."

"It still doesn't feel right."

"Maybe it never will," he said. "Maybe it's not meant to feel 'right.'"

"That's a depressing thought."

He stepped back and turned her to face him. "Things are rarely what you anticipate them being. They just are what they are, and you've got to make the best of it."

"A philosopher cop? Nice."

He smiled. "Since the rest of the family won't get back until later, we have all afternoon to go exploring. That will cheer you up."

"Mom wrote about the Pass of Killiecrankie in her journal."

"I'll take you there. We could both use the fresh air, then we'll head back for a nap. You'll need a rest before meeting the entire family. Boyfriends know best." He winked.

"About that, sorry I didn't correct her."

"Quick thinking on your part. You're catching on."

"That's what worries me. I'm turning into a liar and a flirt."

"No, just a lost girl looking for answers."

A girl who wants you for more than protection.

Damn, she really was an emotional mess. She didn't like having to lean on Bobby Finn. He'd made it clear he had no feelings for her, that their kiss was a result of her "throwing herself at him."

The strange thing was, she'd never felt like that when kissing Steven or anyone else, for that matter.

"I'm going to wash up," he said. "You'll be okay?"

Sheesh, he was afraid she'd fall apart in the few minutes it took him to wash his hands?

"I'm fine." She turned and glanced out the window. He went to the bathroom and shut the door.

She was an emotional mess, sure, but worse, she was depending too heavily on a man again, and this time it was a man who'd be out of her life the moment they landed in the States.

She'd been a good girl her entire life, listened to Dad and followed his suggestions. Her relationship with Steven had fallen into the same pattern. Sure, she cared about him, but it was becoming apparent that she needed him as her touchstone, her stability.

From the window Grace watched Lydia toss garbage out back. The older woman glanced up at Grace, but Grace didn't step away or avoid her gaze. She would not be shamed by this woman. Whatever sins her mother had committed as a teenager didn't belong to Grace.

Lydia pursed her lips; her brows knit together in a sad, almost regretful expression. Then she started walking toward a barn on the far side of the property. About halfway, she turned and motioned with her hand for Grace to join her.

Did she dare?

She'd talk to anyone to get answers. Maybe then she could put the pieces together, figure out why Mom had left and what she was really like as a woman.

Maybe then Grace could find peace.

BOBBY SPLASHED cold water on his face, needing to shock himself back to reality. Studying his reflection in the mirror he noted the few day's growth of beard, rough to the touch.

Yet she'd kissed him anyway.

Splash. Splash. He tried to wash the memory out of his mind.

He could tell she'd wanted to kiss him again just now as they stood by the window overlooking the countryside. She'd wanted to kiss him and he'd barely held on to his self-control.

Not good. Need to get your perspective back, mate.

He had to get control of this thing.

"She has a boyfriend," he said to himself in the mirror.

A boyfriend and she's an emotional wreck. She'd be attracted to any male who offered a shoulder. *It's not like she wants* you, *Bobby Finn.*

No, she had a straight-up bloke waiting for her back home; a boring financial analyst with a daily routine of workouts at his club and fresh salads for lunch. He probably rotated his mattress regularly and bought a new toothbrush every few weeks.

Then there was Bobby, who lived in a constant state of chaos, not knowing where he'd be going next, which murderer he'd be tracking.

For a second he wondered what it would be like to wake up every morning to a fresh-faced girl like

Grace, to go to a boring job and come home to share dinner with her.

The second passed.

"It's a bit fancy for a bloke like me," Bobby said, coming out of the hoity-toity bathroom.

The bedroom was empty. "Bloody Nora," he muttered.

They'd only been apart five minutes, couldn't have been more.

"Grace," he called, hoping she'd materialize from under the bed.

He went into the hallway. "Grace!"

His voice echoed back at him. Racing downstairs, his mind rattled off possibilities. *She's gone down for tea with her cousin, mate. Nothing life-threatening.*

He tried to check the office but it was locked. He poked his head into the empty study, then went to the kitchen. He swung the door open and found Lydia kneading dough.

"Have you seen Grace?" he asked.

"I've seen her."

"Where has she gone?"

With an icy glare, she looked up at him. "She should have gone back to the States. If you really cared about her you'd take her back. This afternoon."

"I tried that already. She needs to find answers."

"She's going to find trouble is what she's going to find. Her mother was trouble and paid for it with her life. Tell the girl to go home and enjoy her nice, safe life. She won't like what she finds here."

"Where is she?"

"I sent her out to the barn." She went back to wrestling with the dough. "She wants answers? She'll find them out there, in her mother's trunk."

"She's not like her mother," Bobby said. "Grace is a sweet girl."

"That will change when she finds out the truth."

Bobby went out the back door and raced to the barn.

That will change when she finds out the truth.

He wouldn't let that happen, wouldn't let her mother's past dim Grace's sparkling personality. She was a sweet, intelligent girl with a warm heart and no ulterior motives. Whatever her mother's sins, Bobby wouldn't let Grace take those on herself.

He pushed open the barn door. "Grace?"

"I'm here."

A shaft of sunlight streamed through a top window, lighting Grace as she sat on the floor. Photographs and papers filled her lap. A black trunk lay open in front of her.

He approached and she glanced up, a lost expression on her face. "Mom's stuff."

"Anything interesting?"

She didn't answer, but held up a newspaper clipping from 1972. The headline read, Bloody Sunday.

"That was a very bad day," he said.

"But why would she have this in her trunk?"

He knelt next to her. He could tell from the look in her eyes that the possibility of her mum being involved with the PIRA was starting to sink in.

"I don't believe it," she whispered.

"It's nice outside, Grace. Let's take a drive," he suggested, afraid of what else she would find.

"And there's this." She handed him a photograph of a group of young people.

"That's my mom." She pointed to a girl, her hair in a ponytail, wearing a big smile.

"She's almost as cute as you."

"Her friend, the boy on the right? He was arrested." She handed him another newspaper clipping featuring a mug shot of the same dark-haired boy.

"That doesn't mean anything, Grace."

"Thanks for trying." She glanced back at the pile of clippings and photographs.

He took her hands in his. "You can make up stories in your mind or you can wait to speak with your aunt and uncle tonight at dinner. They'll tell you the truth, good or bad. This—" he motioned to the trunk and its contents "—is just torturing yourself. Come on, luv, it's an excellent day for a hike."

He placed the photographs and clippings back in the trunk and shut it, then pulled her to her feet.

"I don't get you," she said.

"What, you don't think I'm the out-of-doors type?"

"You act like…"

"Like a bossy wanker? I know. It's a bad habit of mine, always ordering people around." He started walking, hanging on to her hand, taking pleasure in its warmth. Her warmth. He would not let this girl be destroyed by her mother's sins.

"You don't have to do this," she said, as they stepped out of the barn into the sunshine.

"I don't have to take you out to see the country-side? What else would you have us do? Sit in our room and read all afternoon? How bloody boring."

"I meant you don't have to keep trying to cheer me up," she clarified.

He squeezed her hand and kept walking. "Do you need anything from the room?"

"No," she said. "I could use something to eat, though."

"We'll grab lunch on the way out of town."

"Where are you taking me today, Mr. Finn?"

"Well, Miss Fairmont." He smiled at her. "I hear there's a spectacular place just north of town called the Pass of Killiecrankie."

They walked to the car and he opened the door for her. She hesitated and looked into his eyes. "I'm glad you're here." She smiled and slid into the passenger seat.

He shut the door, struggling with the thought of an entire afternoon walking the countryside with Grace beside him, because, truth was, he was more than *glad* to be with her.

He felt whole when helping her, as though all his past failings were washed away every bloody moment he looked into her crystal-blue eyes.

Don't look too much, Finn. It's only an illusion.

"IT'S AMAZING," she said, her eyes widening as they started up the trail, her camera bag over her shoulder.

They were surrounded by lush green forest. The sound of the River Garry rushing through a deep gorge below echoed through the pine and birch trees.

He was glad he'd brought her here. It seemed to have brightened her spirits a bit. She'd eaten little of her sandwich at lunch, even with his encouragement. There was too much going on, she'd said. Too much upheaval.

Like the upheaval in his chest whenever he let his gaze linger too long on her beautiful face?

They strolled along the trail, the sounds of nature making this a serene experience, surreal even. He couldn't remember the last time he'd been in a forest; his work always kept him in crowded, noisy cities.

"There's an attraction up ahead called Soldier's Leap," he said. "The story goes that a fleeing soldier leapt between two rocks and eluded his enemy."

She nodded, smiled. He wished she'd say something.

Now, there's a first. Bobby Finn actually wanting a woman to speak.

They walked a bit and reached The Pass.

"Wow," she said, standing on the very rock the soldier had jumped from. "It's so quiet out here."

He was thinking the same thing. Quiet and peaceful.

Actually perfect, with Grace standing slightly above him, the thick forest framing her face, the slight wind tossing her hair about her cheeks.

"What?" she said with a laugh.

"Nothing," he said, embarrassed that he'd been caught again so obviously admiring her. "There are other places like this close by, Blair Castle, for instance. Here, let me take your photograph."

She handed him her camera bag and he snapped a few shots. He wanted to ask for copies, but didn't.

She stared into the water below and took a deep breath. "It's so peaceful."

"I'm glad you like it."

"Does your job keep you in the city?"

"Mostly, but our last case took us to a small coastal town off the Pacific Ocean."

"What was it about?"

"A boy had gone missing. Authorities thought he'd drowned, but our team wanted to pursue the kidnapping angle."

"I'm almost afraid to ask, did it turn out okay?"

"Yes, actually. We found the boy, no thanks to me."

"Sore subject?"

"A bit. I looked right into the eyes of the man who was blackmailing the family and didn't have a clue he was the culprit. I hate being fooled like that."

"I know the feeling."

He eyed her. "Who fooled you?"

"My father, for one. He should have told me about Mom's dark past long before now."

"He was trying to protect you."

"He lied."

"He didn't lie exactly, he just withheld information. There's a difference."

"Sure, okay, if you say so." She turned to look across the river.

"I've made you cross," he said. "I'm sorry."

She had enough to deal with, poor girl. His job was to protect her and keep her happy.

Admit it, mate, keeping her happy has little to do with this job at this point.

A sound echoed from a mass of trees behind him. He jumped in front of Grace, shielding her.

"What was that?" she said.

"Probably a fox." He eyed the dense grove. "Ready to go back?"

"Sure," she said, as if she sensed danger beyond the trees.

He led her up the path to the rental.

"My camera," she said. "I left it back there."

"Get in the car. I'll go fetch it."

"But—"

"Stay in the car, Grace. I'll be right back."

"Bobby—"

He shut the door on her protest. Walking back to retrieve the camera, he scanned the woods looking for anything out of place: bright colors, something reflective.

Don't see danger where there isn't any, mate.

Yet Bobby could feel the threat, be it human or wild animal. He grabbed hold of the camera-bag strap and straightened.

A click echoed behind him. "Don't turn around."

Blast, he was right to trust his instincts. Bobby raised his hands.

"Good chap." A set of hands patted him down, searching, he presumed, for a weapon, while the barrel of a gun pressed against the back of his head.

"I'm not armed," Bobby said.

Someone affixed a blindfold to his eyes. They were terrorists, out to kidnap him? No, he couldn't be taken away from Grace. *They're probably going to take her, too, mate.*

He grabbed the bastard's wrist and spun around, but the gunman knocked Bobby across the back of the head and he went face-down to the wet earth.

He couldn't see, didn't know how close they were, where the barrel of the gun was pointed.

But he could guess.

Stupid, bloody fool. You never should have left her.

"Can we be gentlemen about this, Mr. Finn?"

"What do you want?" Bobby said.

"The girl, what does she know about her mother?" It was a woman's voice this time.

"You're with the PIRA?" Bobby said.

Someone kicked him in the gut. "Don't ask questions. Answer them," the man said.

"She doesn't know anything," Bobby coughed. "She didn't even know her mother."

"Then why is she here?" the woman asked.

"It's a bloody soul-searching mission."

Silence.

"She's trying to find herself, to find some sort of emotional peace before she moves on with her life," he continued.

"She's in danger," the woman said.

"No bloody kidding."

He thought he'd get another kick for that, but didn't.

"That smart-aleck attitude could get you killed."

"Bobby!" Grace called from the car.

"Don't answer her," the man ordered.

"Leave her alone," Bobby said. "She doesn't know anything."

The barrel of the gun pressed against his temple. "And neither do you. You didn't see us, this didn't happen."

"I understand."

"Smart chap. Now, if you're really that smart,

you'll lie quite still and keep your eyes closed." The blindfold was ripped off. "If you move, we'll track you down and kill you both."

Chapter Twelve

Stay in the car, he'd ordered her.

Ordered. And Grace wasn't taking orders anymore. She could go back and get her own darned camera. She'd forgotten it. "He's just trying to be a gentleman," she whispered.

She headed back up the trail, pepper spray in hand. "Bobby?" He didn't answer. He surely had to hear her. "Bobby, answer me!"

She was getting angry, worried and a bit scared.

Her pulse raced as she forged farther up the trail, paying close attention to her surroundings; the birds chirping, the wind whistling through the trees. She heard a man and woman chatting up ahead. They were off in the distance, and she could only see their backs as they continued along the trail. Is that what she and Bobby had heard? Other tourists?

A few hundred feet down the trail she spotted something bright green in the woods. The shirt she'd bought Bobby as a joke. He'd put it on this morning.

"Bobby," she whispered and went to his side.

She kneeled beside him and noticed a bump at the base of his skull. "My God, what happened?"

He opened his eyes, squinting at first. Then he sat up and glanced around. "I—" He looked at her, then to their surroundings. "I'm not sure."

"Let's get you up." Gripping his arm she helped him stand. His hair was mussed, his eyes glassy and his clothes were covered with mud. "Did you fall or—"

"I don't remember." Panic edged his voice.

Now *he* seemed shaken, spooked.

"Let's go. I'll drive." She led him to the car.

With a deep, fortifying breath she focused on getting him back to the bed-and-breakfast and settling him down. But if he had a concussion, should he rest or be taken to a clinic?

"We'll find a doctor," she said.

"No, I'm fine."

She wasn't going to argue and upset him further, not now, anyway. They drove back to the house and she helped him to the room. He changed into fresh clothes.

"Lie down," she ordered.

"Don't leave," he said as she tucked the blanket over his fully clothed body.

She touched his forehead. He burned.

"I'm always hot, remember?" he explained with a smile.

"I'm worried about you," she admitted.

A second passed. Her hand still touched his face. She wished she could crawl into bed with him, but he'd object for sure.

"I'm going downstairs to get you some ice for the nasty bump on your head."

He didn't let go of her hand. "A cool cloth from the bathroom will be fine. Don't leave, please?"

She went to the bathroom and ran a washcloth under cold water. Glancing into the mirror, she realized she could probably use a rest herself. Her eyes were bloodshot and worry lines creased her forehead.

Walking back into the room, she noticed the clouds had masked the sun outside.

"I think I remember," he said.

She sat on the bed and pressed the cloth to base of his head.

"I lost my footing and slipped. Must have hit my head."

She eyed him. Something didn't feel right. He was lying to her. But why?

"I've got some aspirin," she offered.

"Maybe later. I need to rest. You...you can lie down, as well, if you'd like."

She stretched out beside him, staring at the plaster ceiling and wondering why this felt so comfortable, especially when she knew he was keeping something from her.

"Can I ask a favor?" she said.

"What kind of favor?"

"Please, don't lie to me. Ever. Can you do that?"

"No."

"No?" She turned and their faces nearly touched. "What do you mean, 'no'?"

"My first priority is to keep you safe. If I must lie to do that, then I will."

"But I need to be able to trust you."

"You can. Just know I'm always looking out for your best interest."

"My best interest is the truth," she said, her gaze drifting to his full lips.

"Your best interest is staying safe."

"I've been safe my whole life," she whispered. "But have I lived?"

He glanced back at the ceiling.

She reached out and guided his eyes to meet hers. "Why are you so afraid of me?"

He didn't answer, just stared at her with that lost expression. She pressed her cheek to his chest and closed her eyes.

BOBBY AWAKENED a few hours later. Something ached inside his chest as he felt Grace's body against his. He couldn't believe she'd snuggled up to him with such complete trust, especially since he sensed she knew he was hiding something.

No one had had that much faith in him. Well, no one besides, maybe, Max Templeton.

Not telling her about the assault by the mysterious couple was the right thing to do, at least until he determined who had attacked him, who had asked questions about Grace. Terrorists would have killed him for sure, which meant they were MI5 agents, didn't it? He needed more help from the Blackwell Group, more background information to help him piece this together.

But when could he call in? If he was to keep Grace safe by sticking with her every minute of the day, there wouldn't be much opportunity to call and ask Eddie for research specifics about Grace's mum, the PIRA and MI5. With any luck, Eddie would call Bobby with some news.

In the meantime they were safe here in bed.

At least Grace was safe. Bobby, on the other hand, was at high risk of losing his heart.

He lay there, wide awake, trying to make sense of things. It didn't tally: her mother's involvement with the PIRA, having Grace, leaving her behind. Unless it was because she loved Grace so much. Bobby didn't understand how that worked, but parents were known to do incredibly selfish things and claim love for their child motivated their actions.

He thought about that, thought about what would make her mum leave. No, he couldn't understand it, unless the child was bad, like Bobby, or in danger.

From the PIRA.

Blast, that's it. Her mum had left to protect her.

But why would the PIRA even care about Grace's mum, a woman who had died twenty years ago? It made no sense.

Unless her mum had had something on the group, something that could destroy them.

But they weren't active these days. They were more into discussions than bombings.

He thought about the man in the woods telling Bobby to take her back to the States. It almost seemed as if he cared about keeping Grace safe, not as if he wanted to harm her. Which meant?

Bobby's head ached the more he tried to puzzle through it.

Grace stretched across him, claiming his body with an arm over his chest. He couldn't move, could hardly breathe, the pressure of her arm seeping through his shirt to his skin and deeper still.

The clock on the dresser read six.

"Gracie?" he said.

"Hmm?"

"We've got an hour until supper. Maybe we should think about getting ready?"

"Okay." She didn't move.

"Or not," he whispered. Truth be told, he could lie here all night, content, with Grace leaning into him.

Someone knocked softly on the door. Grace didn't budge. Bobby slipped out from beneath her and cracked open the door.

Anne smiled at him. "Did you two have fun out at Killiecrankie?"

"Yes, thank you."

"We're getting ready for dinner. You may come early if you'd like. Mum was so excited to hear about Grace." Anne strained to peek in the room.

"She's asleep," Bobby said, not sure why he felt the need to protect her from her own family.

"Right, well, do come down soon. My parents are so anxious to speak with her."

"Thank you. We will."

She walked down the hallway, turning once to smile again before she disappeared down the stairs. He closed the door. Grace looked up from the bed to smile at him.

His world tipped a bit, and not because of the blow to his head.

"Thanks for the nap."

"Don't thank me." He went to the bed and sat down.

"I haven't slept that well in days," she said. "Having a live, warm teddy bear must have helped."

"Is that all I am to you? A cuddly toy?" he joked.

"You don't really want me to answer that." Her smile faded. "So, let's get ready." She jumped off the bed and raced to the bathroom.

"No fair!" he called.

She poked her head out the door. "We women take longer to make ourselves beautiful." Then she shut it.

Bugger, he wished she was making herself beautiful for him, not to impress long-lost relations. He glanced at the bed, the rumpled spread and tossed pillows. It was going to be a long night if she expected a repeat of this afternoon, both of them sharing the bed, not touching as lovers, not kssing.

No, he'd take a spot on the floor and stretch out. It was safer that way.

He hoped this reunion with her family would be the end of it. Dinner tonight, maybe a day or two after that, Grace spending most of her time with the newly found relatives. *It will be over soon, mate. Then you can get away from temptation.*

THE EVENING went just as she'd imagined: Aunt Rosie and Uncle Gerry showering her with questions and advice. Grace could barely get a word in edgewise.

"And a teacher," Aunt Rosie said. "What a lovely profession."

"I enjoy the kids," Grace said. "But sometimes I think about doing something else."

"Like what?"

"I don't know, something a little more exciting."

"Excitement is highly overrated," Uncle Gerry said.

They were seated at the formal dining table: Aunt Rosie, Uncle Gerry and Bobby were seated across from her, and Cousin Anne and her brother Jimmy were beside her.

Bobby caught her eye every now and then, shooting her a smile of encouragement.

He seemed to be happy for her, happy that she'd reconnected with her family. She didn't read melancholy or sadness in his eyes for his own loss. She suddenly realized how painful this must be for him.

"I was wondering why the family moved here," Grace said.

The room grew silent.

Aunt Rosie forced a smile. "Your mum had some bad friends in Ireland. Our parents thought it best to move the family to another part of the U.K. They learned about this bed-and-breakfast, that it was up for sale and we moved. It's simple, really."

"Tell us about America, Grace," Jimmy said, forking up a boiled potato. "Is it exciting?"

"I guess that depends what you consider exciting," she said.

Jimmy seemed close to Grace's age, but looked younger with his youthful face and exuberant smile. He had narrow green eyes and full lips and didn't look like anyone in the family.

"Jimmy's into motorbikes and parasailing," his mother scoffed.

"Boy, you really are into excitement," Grace said.

The family chuckled. Laughter, teasing, conversation. All the things she'd never shared with a family, with blood relations. Sure her half-sisters were sweet, but they were ten years younger; Grace hardly shared a sense of humor with them.

They chatted all the way through the entrée

and dessert. Uncle Gerry fired off questions about Grace's upbringing and her childhood. It was as if he was trying to piece together the years lost in not knowing his niece.

Did she remember her mother?

Did her father say where they met?

Did her father know why Mary had come back to the U.K.?

"Enough, Gerry," Aunt Rosie said.

Tea was being served when Grace felt the need to ask the question she'd been avoiding all night.

"Aunt Rosie, you said Mom was involved with a bad crowd. Is it true she was involved with the Provisional Irish Republican Army?"

"We're not sure." Aunt Rosie stood and started clearing dishes. "Help me, Gerry. I'll put the tea on."

Cousin Anne started to get up.

"No, you sit and talk to your cousin," Aunt Rosie said.

Grace glanced at Bobby, who watched her aunt and uncle clear dishes in silence. They went into the kitchen, the door swinging closed behind them.

Cousin Anne faced her. "She doesn't like talking about her sister's activities in the PIRA. It was very hard on the family, not knowing if she was alive or dead, worrying about her day and night. They didn't know where she went when she lived in the States."

"I have a hard time with all this," Grace said. "I always thought of Mom as being such a loving family woman. That is until I learned she abandoned Dad and me long before she died."

"You don't remember her, do you?"

"Not at all."

"She had a bright smile, like yours. I've seen pictures. Did she leave you any pictures to remember her by? Any keepsakes?"

"A locket. Her journal."

"How lovely. What did she write about?"

"Me, as a baby. This place. I mean, Scotland: the hills, the castles, the lochs."

"But nothing about her family? Or friends?"

"No, nothing like that."

"I'm going to help with the tea," Jimmy said.

Bobby narrowed his eyes and watched her cousin leave. Grace watched Bobby. She knew that look, that suspicious look. What was the deal?

"Grace, it would make my mother feel so much better if she knew she'd been remembered in her sister's diary. Was there nothing about her? Or her parents?"

"No, I'm sorry. She wrote exclusively about me, a little about my dad and a lot about Scotland. She loved this country."

"Yes, I'm sure." Anne's voice drifted off.

Aunt Rosie floated in with the tea, followed by Uncle Gerry with mini-cakes. They continued their conversation about Grace's life and potential future.

"What about a serious boyfriend?" Aunt Rosie said, winking at Bobby.

"No, we're not," Grace paused, "serious." Her gaze caught Bobby's. His brows furled together in question.

"I'm not ready," Grace admitted.

Not ready to marry Steven, the wrong man. It felt as if a weight had been lifted from her shoulders. Admitting the truth to herself was a huge relief.

"Well, don't wait too long," Rosie said. "Let's sit in the front room, shall we?" She stood and they all followed her into the delightful room with a fireplace centered on the far wall.

They chatted and told stories, mostly about Grace's mother as a child, but nothing about Mom after the age of seventeen, Grace noted. Were they all ashamed of her? Maybe, but they seemed to accept Grace unconditionally.

While Anne had said she was readying the rooms for guests earlier, Grace hadn't heard anyone enter or leave tonight. Maybe they had romantic couples checking in, wanting their privacy.

She glanced at Bobby, whose intense stare made her want to shift position in the highback chair. He was studying her, almost as if he was trying to read her mind. He jumped to his feet. "I'll be right back."

She looked at him in question, but he didn't make eye contact. Odd.

She and the ladies continued their storytelling, while Uncle Gerry smoked his pipe. Jimmy had been absent since dessert, probably fearing he'd be bored to tears by the conversation. He seemed the wild sort, but playful. A bit like Bobby Finn.

As she leaned back and enjoyed the camaraderie, she realized this was what she'd been looking for: this connection to relatives, the unconditional acceptance, maybe even love.

"You'll be staying with us for how long, then?" Aunt Rosie asked.

"I guess that depends on how long you'll have me."

Aunt Rosie gave her a strange look.

"Just kidding," Grace said. "I plan to stay a week in Scotland, maybe a few days in London before I return home."

"You're welcome to stay longer," Aunt Rosie offered.

Uncle Gerry shot her a look, probably dreading more nights of sitting around listening to women's chatter.

"Thanks, that's a nice thought," Grace said. "But I do have things to get back to." Like breaking up with my boyfriend. Yikes. How was she going to explain that? *You're a nice guy, Steven, but now that I've found some peace in my life, I no longer need to depend on men like you to make me feel whole?*

"It's been lovely to meet you," Aunt Rosie said.

"Same here." Grace smiled, feeling a new connection to her mother.

The door burst open. Grace turned to see Bobby marching into the room, his hands raised.

"Sit down," Cousin Jimmy said, shoving at Bobby from behind.

That's when Grace saw the gun. Her blood ran cold.

"Sorry, Gerry," Jimmy said to his father. "The bloke found me making a copy of her diary."

"Wait, what?" Grace demanded.

"This isn't real, Grace, it's a set-up," Bobby said. "My guess is they're British Intelligence. They're not your blood relations any more than I am."

Chapter Thirteen

Grace's heart split in two as she struggled to process Bobby's words.

"British Intelligence?" she repeated.

"Your mother was on our watch list," said Anne, the person who she'd formerly thought was her cousin. "She was a high-ranking member of the PIRA and a new, radical group has been formed in her honor. Your mother had stolen a list of MI5 agents. She died before we could get it back."

"You killed her?"

Anne glanced at Uncle Gerry. Or rather, not Uncle Gerry. He shook his head.

"You did, didn't you?" Grace pushed.

"We didn't have her killed," Gerry said. "That was her own doing."

"You bloody twit," Jimmy said to Bobby. "You've complicated everything because you're trying to be clever. I'll wipe that clever grin off your face." He raised his hand to hit Bobby.

Grace jumped to her feet. "Stop!"

"Enough!" Gerry commanded.

Jimmy's face turned red as he stared down at Bobby, who returned the man's gaze with cold, hard eyes.

"All lies," Grace said.

Bobby got up to go to her, but that bastard Jimmy pushed him back to his chair. Bobby couldn't stand the look of confusion in her eyes.

She glanced at each person in the room, one by one. "None of you are related to me, are you?"

"No," Anne said. "I'm sorry, but the truth is your boyfriend is with MI5, as well."

Grace leaned against the sofa. "Steven?"

"An agent assigned to befriend you," Rosie explained.

"No wonder I've been keeping an emotional distance," she whispered. "I felt something wasn't right."

Silence filled the room. Bobby wanted to comfort her but he sensed she needed space, time to process.

She looked at Gerry. "I haven't been imagining things. Steven's here, in Scotland."

"He's been keeping watch over you, yes."

Her gaze drifted to the floor. She seemed devastated. Bobby wanted to slug someone.

She pinned Gerry with a cold stare. "What happened to Mom's family?"

"No one knows."

"Ah, no one knows," Grace said, defeat coloring her eyes. "This, this was all a big game to you, manipulating my feelings and acting as though you cared about me."

"We needed information," Anne said. "We think the radicals are after it, as well. Your life may be in danger."

An odd chuckle escaped Grace's lips.

Bobby gripped the arms of his chair. Was she going to have a breakdown?

"Are you done? With me?" Grace looked Gerry directly in the eye.

"After we get a copy of the diary, yes."

"Fine." She walked toward the door, hesitated and turned. "So, you're with British Intelligence and you have no idea where my mother's family is?"

"I'm sorry," Rosie said.

"British Intelligence," Grace repeated. "Now there's an oxymoron if I've ever heard one." She left the room, seemingly in control, yet Bobby sensed the storm brewing. She'd been lied to, manipulated and played like a harp.

Bobby stood to follow her. Jimmy shoved the barrel of his gun in Bobby's face. "Where do you think you're going?"

"Listen, you wanker, you four just built her up and tore her down to pieces. I'm not going to sit here and watch her fall apart because of an old score you have with her mum. You're paid to be heartless, I'm paid to protect. Now get the hell out of my way before I rip your arm out of its socket."

"You really think you can do that, mate?" Jimmy taunted.

"Enough!" Gerry ordered. Jimmy lowered his gun. "There's more to this than her mother's involvement with PIRA," Gerry explained.

"Gerry, don't," Rosie warned.

"He needs to know if he's going to protect her." He looked at Bobby. "Grace Fairmont's mother was recruited by British Intelligence in the seventies for the purpose of infiltrating the PIRA."

"She was an MI5 agent?" Bobby couldn't believe it.

"Yes. As an undercover agent she'd told the PIRA about a list she had of MI5 agents. She was using this to work her way up the ranks. She died before they could get it from her, and now there's a new radical branch that's out to find the list and use it against England."

"But it was a fake list, yeah?" Bobby said.

"We gave her a list to use, but unbeknownst to us, a traitor in MI5 printed out the real names of agents. Once she discovered what she had, Mary couldn't pass the names. If she passed false names to PIRA, they could check with their insider and she'd be dead. She was compromised. She," he hesitated, "died in the bombing. PIRA never fully believed she died."

And Bobby wondered himself.

"Would you tell me if she were still alive?"

Gerry sighed. "She's not. But know this, everything Mary Logan did, she did because she loved her daughter and wanted to protect her."

"But why is PIRA interested in Grace?" Bobby said.

"They weren't. Until she came looking for her mother's past. The truth is, Mary Logan was a spy before she came to America. We sent her there on another mission. She fell in love, had a child and panicked that she'd be putting the girl in danger by being a part of her life. Mary left America and her daughter to break all ties, to keep the girl safe. She was an honorable woman."

"And a good agent," Rosie added.

"You were the ones on the path this afternoon," Bobby said.

"Yes," Gerry said. "We were hoping our threats to kill her would encourage you to take her back to the States."

"I would like nothing better. But you've seen how determined she is."

"You can't tell her about her mother being MI5," Anne said.

"Excuse me?"

"It will put her in even more danger. If she knows, Grace's questions will only bring things to the surface again."

"The radicals are hoping to find Mary Logan's list," Gerry explained. "They want to use it to raise money to revitalize their cause by selling it to our enemies."

"Good God."

"If we find the list there will be no reason for this new group to pursue Grace. We'll get our advantage back. And as long as you two are here with us you're safe."

Bobby struggled to make sense of it all. *The only thing that matters is keeping her safe.*

Bobby left to find Grace and he ran into Lydia in the hallway. "She's outside," she said, her voice softer, more compassionate than before.

"Where?"

"I gave her a cup of hot tea and a blanket and sent her to the barn to sit with her mother's things." Lydia touched his arm. "I'm not with the others," she said, then smiled. "Her family were good people."

He pushed through the back door into the cool night. Heading for the barn, his mind filled with confusion. Would she ever be safe? Or would protecting her be his job forever?

He could think of worse assignments.

He entered the barn. A small lantern lit the corner where she sat on a blanket.

She glanced up as he approached. "Lydia said... she said everything in here is for real. I'm not sure if that makes me feel better or worse."

"Grace," he started, then went blank. What could he say?

"What does it matter anymore?" She tossed a pearl-handled comb back into the trunk.

"I know what matters." He shifted to the ground beside her. She glanced up into his eyes with a lost, yet angry expression. "What matters is how you see yourself, love," he said, fingering her hair behind her ear.

"I don't know who I am, even less than I did when I started this trip." She pinned him with her sad blue eyes. "I feel disconnected from everything. My dad lied to me, my mom was not what I thought she was, these people—" she glanced at the house, "—used and manipulated me, for what? To get a look at my mother's journal because she was a terrorist. Nothing in my life feels real."

Then her eyes were on him again. "Except you. This." She leaned forward and kissed him. He held her shoulders and broke the kiss.

"Grace, this isn't right."

"Don't push me away."

"I have to."

"Why? Because…because I'm a fool, right? Because I'm such a stupid girl that I was fooled by my father, by those people in there, even by Steven? My God, would he have married me for his job?"

She stood and paced to the other side of the barn. "The way he pretended to care about me, the way he touched me." She shivered. "Yeah, you're right not to fall for a girl like me. A complete idiot."

"Stop it." He went to her.

"Why? It's true. You're probably snickering with the rest of them at the stupid American girl."

"Don't say that. You're bright, and witty and beautiful. I can't kiss you because I want you so badly I won't stop there. I want to drive myself into you, possess you in every way possible, and even then it won't be enough. I've never wanted to possess a woman like that." He caught his breath. "I don't want you to be hurt."

"You won't hurt me."

"You will be hurt. Those bloody terrorists will hurt you right in front of me because I'm distracted by how I feel about you. Let's get into the house where we'll be safe."

He took her hand and led her out of the barn, across the green grass to the house. They went upstairs to their room, seeing no sign of the others.

He couldn't believe he'd so completely lost it, had confessed how he felt about her and what he wanted to do to her. But she didn't seem put off by his outburst. He didn't read fear or apprehension in her eyes.

No, the reflection of desire sparkled back at him. Bloody hell.

He stood by the window, staring up at the stars, when he heard Grace close the bathroom door behind her. He would do anything to ease her pain.

The poor girl deserved so much more out of life than being lied to by the people around her. She deserved to be loved and respected. It seemed an easy assignment for Bobby. Too easy.

A few minutes later she came out of the bathroom wearing a nightshirt. She padded to the bed and climbed under the covers. He reached over, turned off the night lamp and went back to his spot by the window. He wasn't going to get any sleep tonight.

"Bobby?" she said.

"Yes?"

"Would you...would you mind lying with me?"

You wanted to know how to ease her pain, well, this is it, mate. All she wants is a warm body beside her in bed, not to feel so bloody alone. It's a small request.

He sat on the edge of the bed and took off his shoes. Arms behind his head, he stretched out beside her, on top of the covers.

They lay there, bodies touching through the bedding, for a good five minutes. Then she turned over and pressed her cheek against his chest. He thought he'd break apart inside.

Suddenly she shifted up in bed and kissed him.

It started as a sweet kiss, a kiss of thanks, but he couldn't control himself and opened to her, wanting more, needing to taste her.

He broke the kiss. "I'm sorry."

"I'm not," she said, kissing him again, practically climbing on top of him.

He wanted to tell her to stop, that she was on the verge of falling apart and was turning to him not because she wanted Bobby, but because she wanted somebody.

Isn't that what his one-night affairs had always been? For the few hours he'd spent between the sheets with a woman, their bodies tangled and humming with sex, he'd forgotten how empty he felt inside.

Which is probably how Grace felt right now; empty.

And she was turning to Bobby to fill her up, with hope.

He'd do this one thing for her, tonight, and never again. He'd surrender himself to whatever she needed of him. Completely.

NOTHING MADE SENSE anymore. Everyone had lied.

What *was* real?

This, she thought, kissing Bobby Finn. His lips were warm and soft and opening to her with such need.

What had he said? That he wanted to drive himself inside her and even then it would never be enough?

She suspected he hadn't meant to say it, but she knew exactly how he felt.

She'd been drawn to him from the first time they'd met on the train. There had been something tender and loving in his eyes: something genuine.

Pulling his shirt from the waistband of his jeans, she caught him watching her, his eyes half-closed, his lips curved in a subtle smile. She pulled his shirt up and over his head, admiring his firm, slightly hairy chest.

He could have taken the lead, but she suspected he'd had his share of women and knew exactly how to pleasure them. Instead, he lay with arms stretched to his sides, letting her have her way with him, being the gentleman.

Her life was in shambles, yet there was one thing she knew for certain: what she felt for Bobby Finn was real and it was more than simple lust. She'd made an emotional connection to him that first day he'd comforted her on the train. She'd recognized his tender nature beneath the jokes he'd used to cover his pain.

She slipped off her nightshirt, exposing herself to him. "Bobby," she whispered, as she pressed kisses against his chest and down to his stomach. She unsnapped his jeans and slid them off, his need obvious, exciting her. Heat pooled between her legs.

She touched him and he moaned, his right hand clenching the sheets as if he struggled not to lose control. Yet she wanted him to lose control. She wanted him stripped of pretense and politeness. She wanted to know that his intensity matched her own.

Sliding up his body, skin-to-skin, she nibbled and kissed her way to his lips, kissed him once, then broke the kiss and said, "Touch me."

It must have been the permission he'd been waiting for, because he rolled her onto her back and straddled her, his gaze taking in her breasts with a twinkle in his dark-brown eyes. He leaned forward and nuzzled her left nipple and she cried out, grabbing his silk boxer shorts and pulling them down, off his butt.

He eyed her and smiled. "Wild wench," he teased, then kissed her right breast, taking her nipple into his mouth, his tongue flirting with it, driving her completely insane.

If he didn't bury himself inside her soon, she was going to scream in agony. She gripped his buns with trembling fingers, pulling him closer, letting him know she needed him inside her, now.

But he resisted, the tip of his need teasing at her opening.

"Wait." He leaned across the bed and pulled a condom from his wallet in his jeans.

He tore the foil packet with his teeth. "Allow me," she said, taking it from him.

His eyes widened as she pulled the condom from the packet. She reached down to slide it in place and he clenched his jaw, barely able to control himself.

Yet there was no reason to hold back. They were safe in each other's arms, able to trust completely and love without condition.

"Bobby," she breathed. "Please."

He leaned forward and nuzzled her breast, then closed his mouth over hers, teasing and taunting with his tongue. She opened to him, spreading her legs for encouragement, then she gripped his buttocks and pushed him inside her, crying out as they joined together, the rhythm slow and steady, her body on fire.

He reached between them and gently stroked her sensitive nub. She arched, cried out, and he drove himself deep, just as he'd promised, her body absorbing him completely.

He collapsed against her, his heavy breath warming her skin, filling her heart.

This was real.

This was good.

This was love.

BOBBY HAD NEVER felt this way about another living soul.

He stroked the bare skin of her back, thinking they should get up soon. He glanced at the clock on the nightstand. It read twelve-fifteen.

She was probably exhausted from their marathon night of sex. No, it was more than that. Last night with Grace had been Bobby's first true experience of making love to a woman.

Love.

A complicated emotion, and one he'd never truly felt before.

Did Grace feel the same, or was this a case of finding comfort in a stranger's arms?

Stranger, mate? Is that what you are to her? Possibly. But Grace was no stranger to Bobby, not deep in his soul. She'd peeked into his ugly shadows and had seen his ghosts, yet still she wanted him inside of her.

She was just his job. It would all be over once he got her back to the States.

She stretched and opened her eyes, smiled at him.

"Hey, you," she said, kissing his cheek. Warmth floated across his skin and down his neck to settle around his heart. Nothing would make him feel like this ever again.

At least he'd felt it this once. At least he knew it was possible for him to experience this kind of love. But he didn't want it from anyone else.

He wanted it from Grace.

"What are you thinking?" she said, narrowing her eyes.

"What an amazing woman I have in my bed."

"I'll bet you say that to all your one-night stands." She smiled and placed her cheek to his chest.

His heart broke. Of course, that's what she considered last night. He wouldn't correct her. If that's how she wanted it, he'd go along.

"I hope you know I'm kidding," she whispered against his skin.

He didn't answer, not sure what to say.

Her head popped up and she fixed her eyes on him. "One night of that isn't nearly enough, you know that, right?"

"I couldn't agree more." He smiled, but still wasn't sure where that left him. Was he her sexual playmate or potential boyfriend?

She laid her head against his chest. "I guess this vacation has been a bust."

"A bust?"

"A failure. A disappointment."

"So sorry, Miss Fairmont."

Her head popped up again. "No, not the you-and-me part. I meant the whole soul-searching part. I guess I would have been better off not coming at all." She rested her chin on her upturned palm and glanced lovingly at him. "But then I never would have met you, would I?"

"Probably not."

"Then, it wasn't a complete bust." She blinked and got a faraway look in her eye. "I just can't believe Mom was a terrorist."

She wasn't! he wanted to shout. She was a government agent assigned to infiltrate the PIRA.

He knew the agents were right; if Grace knew the truth she'd start asking questions and put herself in danger. She needed to let this go; she needed to move on.

With or without Bobby. He had to be fine with her decision. Only, he wasn't sure how he was going to keep the secret about her mother from her. She sensed things about him; puzzled out his thoughts.

"You look awfully serious this morning," she said.

"Didn't get my proper night's rest, is all."

"Yeah? You blaming me for that, big guy?"

"Wouldn't think of it, Miss Fairmont."

She sighed. "What do I do now?"

"I'm sorry?"

"British Intelligence thinks PIRA might be after me, but why?"

"That list of agents was never found. PIRA thinks you could lead them to it."

"But I didn't even know my mother, and I surely don't condone her actions."

Bugger, he ached to tell her the truth, that her mother was not a terrorist, but an agent assigned to prevent terrorism.

"Yet, she was my mother." She glanced at him. "No matter what she did, or who she was, she loved me. I guess that's what matters most."

There was a knock at the door. Bobby got up, put on his shorts and jeans and answered it. "Cousin Anne" stood in the doorway.

"Here's the diary," she said. "If you two wouldn't mind, we'd like to talk to you downstairs."

Bobby nodded and shut the door. He handed Grace the diary.

A half hour later they went downstairs, holding

hands, and found the two female agents in the kitchen, sitting at the counter drinking tea.

"I wouldn't mind some of that," Bobby said, searching through the tea bags for a breakfast blend. Grace stayed close to him, ignoring the agents.

Gerry came in through the back door and removed his boots. "Hope everyone slept well," he said.

"We did," Bobby said. Grace blushed and stared at Bobby's tea.

"We've had word from London. The radical group after the agent list is on their way to Pitlochry."

Bobby automatically put his arm around Grace and held her close.

"Which means?" she said, defiance in her voice.

"Which means they are determined. And so are we." He paced to the island opposite her. "We're determined to protect you as well as to find the list."

"I don't have the damn list," she said.

"No, but they don't know that." He glanced at the women. "We've been planning all night and have come up with a strategy."

Bobby clenched his fist. He sensed what was coming and didn't like it.

"Strategy for what?" Grace asked.

"For ending this," Anne said. "For making sure you're safe, even after you go back to America."

"And what would that be?" Bobby pushed.

"Grace meets with Harry Franklin to give him the

list, one that we've provided. We'll take it from there."

"You mean, you eliminate him," Bobby clarified.

Gerry stared him down. "He runs a group of terrorists that could potentially kill thousands. We'll do what's necessary."

"It's dangerous," Bobby said. "She won't do it."

Grace glanced at him, then at Gerry. "Actually, I will. I won't live my life in the shadow of my mother's sins. Stopping these guys, saving lives, will make up for the ones that were lost. It's the right thing to do."

"I can't let you do this, Grace," Bobby said.

Grace turned to Gerry. "What time and where?"

Bobby glared at the bastard. He was going to use Grace's guilt to his advantage. Bobby wouldn't allow it.

"We've already sent a message from your e-mail address asking to meet Harry at Blair Castle this evening, nine o'clock," Gerry said.

"You bastard," Bobby said. "You weren't going to give her a choice."

"Not true. We knew she'd make the right choice."

"You call that the right choice? Hooking her up with a bloody terrorist?"

"She'll be safe. We'll be close by."

"I'll be closer," Bobby said.

"She should do this alone," Gerry said.

"Rubbish. I'm paid to protect her. I'm going with

her." He respected her need to do this and knew she could take care of herself, but he couldn't stand the thought of her being in danger.

"No, Bobby, it's okay." She turned to Gerry. "I hate what you've done, how you've lied and manipulated me. I'm ending it all at Blair Castle. What's the plan?"

"We'll take you up there for a dry run and show you the equipment," Anne said, walking toward her.

"Grace, listen to me—"

"Don't worry," she said, kissing Bobby on the cheek, her blue eyes brightened by their lovemaking.

"I'm coming with you. We've got to talk."

"I need to do this on my own, without leaning on anyone. I'll see you later."

She left the kitchen with Anne.

"No, Grace." He started after her, but Jimmy got him in some kind of fancy headlock.

"Let me go, you bloody beast."

Gerry walked around to face Bobby. "Can't do that, mate. Can't risk you telling her that her mum wasn't a terrorist. She might lose her motivation." Gerry reached over and stuck something into Bobby's arm. The room spun, then faded to black.

Chapter Fourteen

It was well past suppertime when she got back and found Bobby fast asleep. Boy, he must have been exhausted from their night of lovemaking.

She curled up next to him and watched him breathe, slow and steady. He looked so peaceful.

Her stomach was tied in knots. Even after all the preparation, all the explanation of listening devices and exact location of agents, Grace was nervous as hell about luring Harry Franklin in for the capture.

In truth, she now wished Bobby *would* come with her.

"Bobby," she whispered.

He didn't respond. She should try harder to wake him.

Then he'd be more determined to come with and she knew the agents didn't want Bobby messing up the plan. What had Bobby said? That his feelings for her would get in the way of him protecting her?

Her feelings for Bobby would surely distract her if he was with her tonight. No, doing this alone felt right and good.

It would finally put an end to her soul-searching about her mother.

She'd finally have peace.

"I'm going to make it right, Mom," she whispered, and closed her eyes.

She was starting to understand why Mom had left her and Dad—for their own safety. To a certain degree, that's why she was leaving Bobby behind.

To think that there were some sins you couldn't leave behind, no matter how much you wanted to. But Grace would end this chapter of Mom's history by repairing her honor. Then Grace would move on and build a new life, hopefully with the man sleeping beside her.

It was strange, but a rush of excitement filled her chest at the thought of helping track down terrorists. She felt she was doing something honorable for potential victims. She could see why Bobby had chosen the profession he had. He wanted to make a difference and keep people safe.

There was a soft knock and the door cracked open. "We're leaving in fifteen minutes," Anne whispered.

Grace nodded and placed her hand to Bobby's chest. "Be proud of me, Bobby."

HIDING IN CHAPEL RUINS on the property of Blair Castle, Grace anticipated the sound of footsteps. Nerves twisted her stomach into knots.

"Nothing yet," Gerry said through her earpiece.

She tapped her fingers against Mom's diary in her lap. It was a convincing move, to rip a page out of her diary with the false list of agents and hand it to Harry. That would explain why Harry hadn't found the list in her backpack, because her diary hadn't been in the backpack.

The agents had planned everything to the nth degree. She rubbed her thumb against the inside back cover, back and forth, as she'd done so many times when thinking or nervous. Back and forth.

She felt a rough spot, opened the journal and looked closer, using her miniflashlight. The seam had come loose. She peeled back the edge and felt something tucked behind the panel. She pulled out a slip of white paper and opened it.

"Oh, my God," she said, reading a list of names.

"Grace? What is it?" Gerry asked via her earpiece.

"The list."

"It's right there, in Mary's diary."

"No, I mean…" Her voice trailed off as she scanned the list, complete with photos of MI5 agents. She recognized Gerry and Rosie…and Mary Logan.

"She was with British Intelligence?" she whispered.

"Bloody hell, who's that?" Gerry said.

"Gerry, I have the list. Why is my mom on it?"

"Get out, now!" Crackling filled the line.

"Gerry?"

Nothing.

She suddenly felt all alone. And she had the list, a list of MI5 agents that included her mother. Those bastards had lied about that, too.

"Mom, what do I do?"

Mom had been an agent; not a terrorist. She had been a protector, a woman trying to save lives, not take them.

If the real list fell into the wrong hands Mom would be known as a failure, her work would have been for nothing. Abandoning Grace and Dad would have been pointless.

Grace stood, sensing she was on her own, that somehow the agents had been compromised. She wasn't going to sit here and wait for Harry Franklin to kill her.

She heard gravel crunch under a man's boots. Too late. He was here.

Tucking the list in her pocket and the diary at the back of her jeans, she waited, holding the pepper spray in a firm grip. She hoped it had enough power left to paralyze Harry, giving her time to escape.

Harry Franklin stepped into the chapel ruins.

"Harry?" she said.

He turned. She aimed and fired, hitting him

square on. She ran, but he got hold of her jacket and jerked her back.

"You bloody bitch! Get back here!"

Do whatever it takes, Bobby had said.

She grabbed Harry's hair and yanked as hard as she could, smashing his face against the back of her head. It was enough to stun him, enough for her to get away. She stumbled and tripped, but managed to stay on her feet, racing across the grounds. The wind blew her hair across her face as she sprinted toward the woods.

What if they catch you? What will they do to you?

She couldn't think about that, now. Had to get away. Had to tell Dad about Mom, that she was a hero, not a terrorist, that she was—

She tripped on a tree root and went down. She hit the ground with a thud, the wind knocked from her lungs. She heard footsteps closing in. She tried to scramble away, but a hand grabbed her arm and jerked her to her feet. "Keep running," Bobby ordered.

"Bobby?"

Her protector. Her love.

They raced into the forest, Bobby pulling her across the uneven earth deeper into the woods. He squeezed her hand to comfort her.

"Are you hurt?" he said.

"No, I'm—"

A shot rang out and she went into Bobby's arms.

"You're dead if you don't come with me," Harry threatened from behind.

So it had come to this. Harry Franklin and his terrorists against Grace and Bobby.

"Thought you could outwit me?" he said with a cough, stepping closer, aiming the gun at them. "Stupid girl, I should have finished you on the train."

Bobby shielded her.

"Come out from behind him," Harry ordered.

"Don't move," Bobby said to Grace.

"You're going to die for this girl? Why, because she's good in bed?"

"She'll give you the list, then you'll let her go."

"No. We've got some questions about her mum."

"She didn't know her."

"I think she knows more than she's letting on, isn't that right, Gracie?"

Bobby lunged at Harry Franklin. "Run, Grace!" he cried.

She turned and raced into the woods, panic flooding her chest. A gun went off, twice. Tears streamed down her face. She'd just found Bobby, had just fallen in love with him.

And he was protecting her, giving his life to save hers.

She would not get caught by these bastards again.

She jumped behind a fallen tree and burrowed deep against it, hoping Harry would run right past. A few minutes later she heard footsteps crunch against the leaves.

"Grace?"

"Bobby?" She jumped out of hiding and went to him, hugging him.

"Easy now," he said.

She stepped back. Blood was smeared across his jacket and shirt.

"Oh, my God."

"Don't get hysterical. I'm fine," he said. "MI5 showed up. Rosie and Jimmy took Harry away. Let's get back."

He led her out of the woods.

"I can't believe you're here. Bobby, look, I found the real list." She pulled it from her pocket. "And you're not going to believe it but Mom's name is on there. She wasn't a terrorist, she was a British Intelligence agent."

"I know."

"You know?"

"They told me last night."

"You knew she wasn't a terrorist, but you let me believe she did those horrible things?"

"I was trying to protect you."

"I'm tired of people protecting me, always assuming I'm unable to take care of myself."

"They feared if you knew the truth you'd ask more questions, and that would put you in further danger."

"I'm not stupid, Bobby. And believe it or not, I can take care of myself. You lied to me after I specifically asked you to be truthful. What about last night? You made love to me. Why?"

"You know I care about you."

"How do I know that? You lied about my mother. My God, you were the only person I thought hadn't lied, the only person I could trust. You've been playing me like all the rest: Steven, these spies. You're just like them, manipulate the naive Grace Fairmont so you can do your job and get a raise. Well, good job, Bobby Finn, you should get a big one." She spun around to find Anne and Gerry staring at her.

"What?" she said. "I want to go home."

She marched toward them and Anne led her to the surveillance van.

Bobby just stood there. Gerry walked up to him. "Need a hand, mate?"

"No." He gripped his side, where the bullet had grazed his skin. "I'm fine."

Grace glared at him before getting into the van.

Gerry's speculative gaze went between Grace and Bobby, then he said, "Ah, don't worry. She'll come around."

"Not likely." It was then Bobby realized he'd secretly been fantasizing about a future with her.

"What do you mean? You took a bullet for her."

"I also lied to her."

"To protect her."

"She's had people lying to her her whole life. She was depending on me to be truthful."

"Well, she's alive, thanks to you. I think that

trumps a little white lie. But then lying is my business, so what do I know?" He winked.

Bobby got in the back of the van and they headed to the house. Grace sat up front, back straight, mouth shut.

"Sorry about the confusion back there," Gerry said. "Harry Franklin brought more members than we'd anticipated."

"Yeah, it's a good thing Bobby showed up," Anne said.

Grace didn't respond.

"This is finally over," Anne said to Grace.

"And it was all because Mom had this." Grace pulled out a piece of paper and handed it to Anne.

"Good God, you found it!" Anne exclaimed.

"If you're ever interested in becoming a spy—"

"No thanks, *Uncle* Gerry," Grace said. "I have this thing about lying and manipulation."

"Pity."

"Maybe we should drop Bobby at a clinic," Anne suggested.

"I'm fine." He noticed Grace didn't react to the suggestion. Of course not. He was the enemy, a heartless bastard who'd lied to her then bedded her.

As they drove back to the house, Bobby pieced together events of the last few days. The driver who had picked them up at Waverly Station was most likely MI5, along with the two officers who had arrested him. They must have drugged him to get information about Grace, to determine what she knew about her spy mother and if she could lead them to the agent list.

Twenty minutes later they pulled into the drive and got out. Grace walked ahead, aiming for the house, ignoring Bobby.

"Guess you're sleeping on the couch tonight," Gerry chuckled.

"I can't stay here."

"But we've got to patch you up," Anne said.

"Then I'm gone. Can you drive her back to Edinburgh and make sure she gets on a plane?" Bobby asked.

"Sure," Gerry said. "Where are you off to?"

"London to visit some friends. Then back to America."

But his heart would never be the same.

THE NEXT MORNING Grace packed and went in search of something to eat. Bobby had come upstairs last night only briefly to pack his things then he'd left, probably to sleep in a spare room. Good. She still hadn't gotten over his lying to her, but it was damn hard to be mad at him with his bullet wound reminding her he'd risked his life for her.

Of course he had. That was his job.

Well, fine. She was going to do her job and live her own life, surrounded by people she could trust.

She went into the kitchen to find Anne at the counter drinking tea.

"Good morning," she said, and went straight for the teakettle to fill it with water.

"Good thing your friend was there to help out last night," Anne commented.

"My bodyguard," she corrected.

"Yes, well, it's a good thing. He surely cares about you."

"He lies, too," she shot back. "I'm done with liars."

"He kept our secret to protect you."

"I've heard that line so many times these past few days. I'm tired of it." She put on the kettle and searched through boxes of tea.

"Do you know why Bobby was asleep when you left for the mission last night?"

"He was tired." She tried not to blush, thinking about their lovemaking that had tired him out.

"He was drugged."

"What?" She turned to Anne.

"We drugged him because he was going to tell you the truth about your mother being an agent. It would have ruined everything."

"He was going to tell me?"

"Yes, and to hell with national security, or the safety of that list of agents or innocent civilians. He did not want you to go to Blair Castle and risk your life because you felt guilty about your mum's activities. He put you first. We don't have that luxury."

"Whatever. Where is he? I need a ride back to Edinburgh."

"He's gone. Left this morning. We'll get you to the airport."

Bobby was gone. She'd never see him again. She should feel happy, relieved.

But she wasn't. She felt empty inside.

"Did you love Steven?" Anne asked.

Grace snapped her attention to the agent. "What?"

"Did you love him?"

"I…no," she admitted.

"Yet you said the words, didn't you?"

"Yes."

"You lied."

"I was being nice. I…" she hesitated "…didn't want to hurt his feelings."

"And Bobby Finn didn't want to see you hurt. We're all liars at one time or another. The important thing is we know how to love. I don't have the luxury of being in love, not in my line of work." She turned off the kettle, poured hot water into a cup and handed it to Grace. "Just let me know when you're ready and I'll drive you to the airport."

Grace stood there in shock, absorbing Anne's words.

It dawned on Grace that her mother had sacrificed everything because she loved Dad and their baby so much.

Love *was* a gift. But Grace had been so blinded by her pride that she couldn't see past it into Bobby's loving eyes. God, what had she done?

Chapter Fifteen

Bobby didn't waste much time getting back to work. He spent two days in London then flew back to Seattle.

He was off-kilter, jet-lagged and cranky.

Not to mention heartbroken.

"The best remedy is hard work," he said to himself as he took the bus to Blackwell headquarters in Pioneer Square.

He got off at Yesler and went to the office building, glad that his work was the kind that consumed a man's mind completely.

If only it could consume his heart, deaden it to the constant ache.

Grace. How the bloody hell had he let her sneak inside like that? He should have known it would fall apart. He wasn't meant to have a successful relationship with a woman.

He climbed the stairs to the second floor, took a deep breath and pushed open the door.

"Hey, Bobby boy!" Eddie called out. The bloke wore a colorful, collarless T-shirt and tie. "I dressed up for ya." He shook Bobby's hand.

"Thanks, mate."

Jeremy congratulated Bobby, followed by Spinelli and Ramos. It felt good to be back; he felt as if he belonged.

"Excellent job, mate," Max said. "You get bodyguard duty and end up taking on PIRA and MI5. And you kept the girl safe."

"Did my best, guv."

"Brilliant. Well, we've got a new client and I'm in the process of hiring a few new members to round out the team. I thought you might want to review a candidate for office assistant before I offer her the job."

"Guv, I don't know. I'm a detective, not human resources."

Max smiled. "Do it for me, mate."

Bobby glanced into Max's office at a blond girl who sat in front of his desk, shoulder-length waves touching her shoulders. Now Bobby was hallucinating.

In slow motion he went to Max's office and hovered in the doorway. "Hello. I'm Bobby Finn." She stood and turned to him.

Grace. She smiled.

The world went wonky again and he could have sworn there'd been a bloody earthquake.

"Grace, what are you doing here?"

"Come in and shut the door."

He did, but he didn't get close to her for fear she'd disappear.

"I'm here to clarify a few things," she said. "First, you know how I hate when people keep things from me."

"I know, Grace, I was trying to—"

"Wait, let me finish." She took a few steps toward him. She looked fetching this morning in her tight jeans and T-shirt, wearing her favorite denim jacket. "But, the thing is," she said, within inches of him. "I've done the same thing with the people I care about. I lied to Dad, always pretending to be happy and content. I lied to you when I acted brave about taking on Harry Franklin—I was scared, but I didn't want to put you at risk by involving you. Yet you showed up anyway."

She touched his cheek and he closed his eyes.

"And I think I'm going to have to lie again and tell you I'm going to walk out of here and I'll be just fine without you in my life."

He opened his eyes and tried to read her meaning.

"I can do that," she said. "Or I can tell the truth and say I've never felt this way before. That it should scare the hell out of me, but it doesn't because it feels right, and it's something I'd like to pursue."

He didn't know what to say. This was more than he'd imagined, more than he deserved.

"But I get the feeling serious relationships freak you out, so I can lie," she said. "I can do that for you because I love you. And as you've taught me, we sometimes lie to keep loved ones safe, right?"

Completely humbled by her confession, he took her in his arms and held on. "Grace, I don't know what to say. I'm afraid I'll muck it up."

She leaned back and looked up into his eyes. "Have a little faith, Bobby. You'd be surprised what love can do."

* * * * *

Turn the page for a sneak preview of
IF I'D NEVER KNOWN YOUR LOVE
by
Georgia Bockoven

From the brand-new series
Harlequin Everlasting Love
Every great love has a story to tell. ™

One year, five months and four days missing

There's no way for you to know this, Evan, but I haven't written to you for a few months. Actually, it's been almost a year. I had a hard time picking up a pen once more after we paid the second ransom and then received a letter saying it wasn't enough. I was so sure you were coming home that I took the kids along to Bogotá so they could fly home with you and me, something I swore I'd never do. I've fallen in love with Colombia and the people who've opened their hearts to me. But fear is a constant companion when I'm there. I won't ever expose our children to that kind of danger again.

I'm at a loss over what to do anymore, Evan. I've begged and pleaded and thrown temper tantrums with every official I can corner both here and at home. They've been incredibly tolerant and understanding, but in the end as ineffectual as the rest of us.

I try to imagine what your life is like now, what you do every day, what you're wearing, what you eat. I want to believe that the people who have you are misguided yet kind, that they treat you well. It's how I survive day to day. To think of you being mistreated hurts too much. If I picture you locked away somewhere and suffering, a weight descends on me that makes it almost impossible to get out of bed in the morning.

Your captors surely know you by now. They have to recognize what a good man you are. I imagine you working with their children, telling them that you have children, too, showing them the pictures you carry in your wallet. Can't the men who have you understand how much your children miss you? How can it not matter to them?

How can they keep you away from us all this time? Over and over, we've done what they asked. Are they oblivious to the depth of their cruelty? What kind of people are they that they don't care?

I used to keep a calendar beside our bed next to the peach rose you picked for me before you left. Every night I marked another day, counting how many you'd been gone. I don't do that any longer. I don't want to be reminded of all the days we'll never get back.

When I can't sleep at night, I tell you about my day. I imagine you hearing me and smiling over the details that make up my life now. I never tell you how defeated I feel at moments or how hard I work to hide it from everyone for fear they will see it as a reason to stop believing you are coming home to us.

And I couldn't tell you about the lump I found in my breast and how difficult it was going through all the tests without you here to lean on. The lump was benign—the process reaching that diagnosis utterly terrifying. I couldn't stop thinking about what would happen to Shelly and Jason if something happened to me.

We need you to come home.

I'm worn down with missing you.

I'm going to read this tomorrow and will probably tear it up or burn it in the fireplace. I don't want you to get the idea I ever doubted what I was doing to free you or thought the work a burden. I would gladly spend the rest of my life at it, even if, in the end, we only had one day together.

You are my life, Evan.

I will love you forever.

* * * * *

HARLEQUIN® *Romance*®

presents a brand-new trilogy by

PATRICIA THAYER

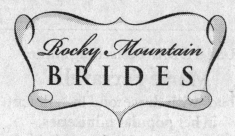

Rocky Mountain BRIDES

Three sisters come home to wed.

In April don't miss

Raising the Rancher's Family,

followed by

The Sheriff's Pregnant Wife,

on sale May 2007,

and

A Mother for the Tycoon's Child,

on sale June 2007.

This February...

Catch NASCAR Superstar *Carl Edwards* in
SPEED DATING!

Kendall assesses risk for a living—so she's the last person you'd expect to see on the arm of a race-car driver who thrives on the unpredictable. But when a bizarre turn of events—and NASCAR hotshot Dylan Hargreave—inspire her to trade in her ever-so-structured existence for "life in the fast lane" she starts to feel she might be on to something!

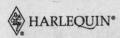

INTRIGUE

COMING NEXT MONTH

#981 SPECIAL ASSIGNMENT by Ann Voss Peterson
Bodyguards Unlimited, Denver, CO (Book 2 of 6)
Mike Lawson is just the type of honest cop needed to protect
Prescott agent Cassie Allen as police corruption overruns Denver.

#982 PRESCRIPTION: MAKEOVER by Jessica Andersen
In order to expose a vast conspiracy, Ike Rombout undergoes a
full makeover that turns her into exactly the sort of girly-girl she
despises—only to catch the watchful eye of investigator William Caine.

#983 A SOLDIER'S OATH by Debra Webb
Colby Agency: The Equalizers (Book 1 of 3)
Spencer Anders joined the Equalizers to start over. But can he recover
Willow Harris's son from the Middle East *and* give Willow a chance at
a new beginning?

#984 COMPROMISED SECURITY by Cassie Miles
Safe House: Mesa Verde (Book 2 of 2)
FBI special agents Flynn O'Conner and Marisa Kelso must confront
their darkest, most personal secrets while pursuing an elusive killer.

#985 SECRET CONTRACT by Dana Marton
Mission: Redemption (Book 1 of 4)
Undercover soldier Nick Tarasov has been after an untouchable arms
dealer for years, but this time he has Carly Jones with him—and she
has nothing to lose.

#986 FINDING HIS CHILD by Tracy Montoya
Search-and-rescue tracker Sabrina Adelante never gave up looking
for Aaron Donovan's daughter. Aaron still believes his daughter is out
along Renegade Ridge, but is he seeking closure—or vengeance?

www.eHarlequin.com

HICNM0307